PRAISE FOR JAYNE ANN KRENTZ'S

DEEP WATERS

"Adventure, humor, romance, and a great supporting cast of characters add up to another very enjoyable novel by Jayne Ann Krentz."

—*Library Journal*

"Highly recommended for anyone feeling the winter blahs. . . . The clever and constant repartee between Charity and Elias is of the laugh-aloud quality without being slapstick. The sexual tension and subsequent lovemaking burn holes in the paper."

—*Bookpage*

"The inimitable style of Ms. Krentz shines supremely in *DEEP WATERS*. The characters are darling and quirky, and the plot is vintage. The reader will be alternately entertained with humor, suspense, lavish sensuality, and all-around great pleasure. Pamper yourselves; this one is worth it."

—*Rendezvous*

"A fun read. . . . Krentz has a real gift for dreaming up unusual characters, and *DEEP WATERS* is up to her usual standards. . . ."

—*The Oakland Press* (Pontiac, MI)

"Krentz fans will be very pleased with her latest. . . . *DEEP WATERS* has everything Krentz fans have come to expect and more. . . . Submerse yourself in an entertaining and satisfying love story."

—*Compuserve Romance Reviews*

"Ms. Krentz does it all well. . . . There is instant tension and mixed feelings between Charity and Elias. . . ."

—*The Chattanooga* (TN) *Times*

"Superb. . . . Quirky humor and passionate romance with a touch of suspense."

—*Romantic Times*

JAYNE ANN KRENTZ'S
PREVIOUS NOVELS

ABSOLUTELY, POSITIVELY

"[A] cheerful escapist package combining sex and mystery. . . ."

—Cosmopolitan

"A delight. . . . Krentz's leads are engaging and believable. . . . It's no wonder that the author's novels consistently hit best-seller lists—as this one should too, absolutely, positively."

—Publishers Weekly

TRUST ME

"As in all Ms. Krentz's books, her characters are colorful, unique individuals who draw the reader into the story immediately. Secondary characters are unusual and amusing. . . . Great fun to read."

—Rendezvous

"The pace is brisk and the high-tech gloss fun. . . . This should please Krentz's readership and may even lure some of her Amanda Quick fans into the 20th century."

—Publishers Weekly

GRAND PASSION

"Filled with the kind of intelligent, offbeat characters . . . [who] are so fun to get to know that it's hard to close the book on them."

—USA Today

"Krentz at her best . . . with the snappy dialogue that has become her trademark and a cast of characters you want to know personally."

—Sandra Brown

Also by Jayne Ann Krentz

Absolutely, Positively
Deep Waters
Eye of the Beholder
Family Man
Flash
The Golden Chance
Grand Passion
Hidden Talents
Perfect Partners
Sharp Edges
Silver Linings
Sweet Fortune
Trust Me
Wildest Hearts

Written under the name Jayne Castle
Amaryllis
Orchid
Zinnia

Published by POCKET BOOKS

For information regarding special discounts for bulk purchases,
please contact Simon & Schuster Special Sales at
1-800-456-6798 or business@simonandschuster.com

JAYNE ANN KRENTZ

DEEP WATERS

POCKET BOOKS
New York London Toronto Sydney Singapore

This book is a work of fiction. Names, characters, places and incidents
are products of the author's imagination or are used fictitiously. Any
resemblance to actual events or locales or persons, living or dead, is
entirely coincidental.

POCKET BOOKS, a division of Simon & Schuster, Inc.
1230 Avenue of the Americas, New York, NY 10020

Copyright © 1996 by Jayne Ann Krentz

ISBN: 0-7434-5722-6

First Pocket Books paperback printing December 1997

10 9 8 7 6 5 4

POCKET BOOKS and colophon are registered
trademarks of Simon & Schuster Inc.

Cover art by Tom Hallman

Printed in the U.S.A.

For my brother,
Stephen Castle,
with love

Prologue: Charity

—◈—

The sea lures the unwary with the promise of freedom,
but it harbors great risk.

— "On the Way of Water," from the journal of Hayden Stone

The panic attack struck as Charity Truitt swept
through the glass-paned French doors of one of the
most exclusive business clubs in Seattle. It hit her with
the force of a stiff jolt of electricity. Her pulse
pounded. She could scarcely breathe. Perspiration suddenly threatened to ruin her outrageously sophisticated red silk dress. Luckily, she hadn't paid retail for
the overpriced scrap of designer whimsy. Her family
owned the store in which it had been on display in
the couture section.

Charity came to a halt in the doorway of the private
lounge that had been reserved for the occasion. She
struggled to take a deep breath. She put up an even
more valiant fight to conceal the fact that she had a
major problem on her hands. It occurred to her that

1

those in the well-dressed crowd who noticed her hovering there on the threshold probably thought she was making an intentionally dramatic entrance. The truth was, she was on the verge of panicked flight.

With the iron-willed discipline of a woman who had been running a corporation since the age of twenty-four, she forced herself to smile while anxiety shredded her insides.

It wasn't the first panic attack she had endured. They had been striking with increasing frequency during the past four months, destroying her sleep, making her edgy and restless, and, worst of all, raising dark questions about her mental health.

The attacks had driven her first to her doctor and then to a therapist. She got some technical explanations but no real answers.

An unprovoked fight-or-flight response, the therapist had said. An evolutionary throwback to the days when we all lived in caves and worried about monsters in the night. Stress was usually a contributing factor.

But now, tonight, Charity suddenly knew the real reason for the attacks. She realized at last what, or, rather, who, triggered the surges of panic. His name was Brett Loftus, owner of Loftus Athletic Gear. He was big, well over six feet tall, and, at thirty, still endowed with the body of the varsity football star he had once been. He was also blond, brown-eyed, and good-looking in an engaging, old-fashioned, western hero sort of way. Just to top it off, he was hugely successful and a really nice man.

Charity liked him, but she did not love him. She was pretty sure that she could never love him. Worse, she had a strong hunch that her stepsister, Meredith, and the easygoing, good-natured Brett were perfect for each other. The recent panic attacks had not diminished all of her near-legendary intuition.

Unfortunately, it was Charity, not Meredith, who was supposed to announce her engagement to the heir to the Loftus empire tonight.

The merger was to be a business move as well as a personal union. In a few weeks, Loftus Athletic Gear would be joining with the family-owned Truitt department store chain to form Truitt-Loftus.

The new company would be one of the largest privately owned retailers in the Northwest. If all went well, it would begin expanding into the exciting Pacific Rim market within two years.

For the sake of the family and business responsibilities that she had shouldered so early, Charity was about to marry a man who gave her anxiety attacks every time he took her into his arms.

It was not Brett's fault that he was so big that she got claustrophobic when he kissed her, she thought wildly. It was her problem. She had to deal with it.

It was her responsibility to solve problems. She was good at that kind of thing. People expected her to take command, to manage whatever crisis happened to present itself.

Charity's hands tingled. She could not get any air into her lungs. She was going to faint, right here in front of some of the most influential and powerful people in the Northwest.

She had a humiliating vision of herself collapsed facedown on the Oriental rug, surrounded by bemused friends, business associates, competitors, rivals, and, worst of all, a few chosen members of the local media.

"Charity?"

The sound of her own name startled her. Charity whirled, red silk skirts whipping around her ankles, and looked up at her stepsister, Meredith.

A long way up.

At twenty-nine, Charity was five years older than

3

Meredith, but she was only five foot four inches tall on her best days. Even the three-inch red heels she wore tonight did not put her at eye level with five-foot-ten Meredith, who was also wearing heels.

Statuesque and crowned with a glorious mane of strawberry-blond hair, Meredith was always a stunning sight. Never more so, however, than when she was dressed to the teeth, as she was this evening. No one, Charity thought wistfully, could wear clothes the way her stepsister did.

With her strong, classical features and subtle air of sophistication, Meredith could have made her living as a professional model. She had actually done some in-store fashion work for the Truitt chain during her college days, but her savvy talent and her love of the family business had propelled her straight into management.

"Are you all right?" Meredith's light, jade green eyes narrowed in concern.

"I'm fine." Charity glanced around quickly. "Is Davis here?"

"He's at the bar, talking to Brett."

Unable to see over the heads of the people who stood between her and the club bar, Charity peered through cracks in the crowd. She managed to catch a glimpse of her stepbrother.

Davis was a year and a half older and three inches taller than Meredith. A deeply ingrained flare for retailing and boundless enthusiasm for the Truitt chain had defined his career path, also. Charity had recognized his abilities from the start. Six months ago she had decided to ignore whining accusations of nepotism and promote him to a vice presidency in the company. It was a *family* business, after all. And she, herself, had become president at an extraordinarily early age.

Davis's hair was the same arresting shade as his

sister's, and his eyes were a similar pale green. The colors and the height had come from Fletcher Truitt, Charity's stepfather.

Charity had received her own dark auburn hair and hazel eyes from her mother. She had few memories of her biological father. A professional photographer, Samson Lapford had abandoned his family when Charity was three years old to travel the world shooting pictures of volcanoes and rain forests. He had been killed in a fall while trying to get a close-up of a rare fern that only grew on the sides of certain South American mountains.

Fletcher Truitt was the only father Charity had ever known, and he had been a good one. For his sake and the sake of her mother, she had done her best to fill his shoes since their deaths five years before and hold the family inheritance together for her step-siblings.

The crowd shifted slightly, allowing another view of the bar. Charity saw Brett Loftus, sun-bright hair gleaming in the subdued light, broad shoulders looking even more massive than usual in a tux. A good-natured Norse god of a man, he lounged with negligent ease next to Davis.

Charity shuddered. Once again all the oxygen in the room seemed to disappear. Her palms were so damp she dared not dry them on the expensive fabric of her gown.

Davis was big, but Brett was huge. Charity told herself that there were any number of women in the room who would have traded their Truitt credit cards for a chance to be swept off their feet by Brett Loftus. Sadly, she was not one of them.

The reality of what was happening sent a shock wave through her. With searing certainty she suddenly knew that she could not go through with the engagement, not even for the sake of her step-siblings' inheritance, the altar on which she had sacrificed the past five years of her life.

"Maybe you need a glass of champagne, Charity." Meredith took her arm. "Come on, let's go join Brett and Davis. You know, you've been acting a little strange lately. I think you've been working too hard. Maybe trying to combine the merger with your engagement plans was a bit too much. Now there's the wedding to schedule and a honeymoon."

"Too much." The panic was almost intolerable. She would go crazy if she didn't get out of here. She had to escape. "Yes. Too much. I have to leave, Meredith."

"What?" Meredith started to turn, an expression of astonishment on her face.

"Right now."

"Calm down, Charity. What are you saying? You can't just run off. What would Brett think? Not to mention all these people we've invited."

Guilt and the old steely sense of duty swamped Charity. For a few seconds, the combination did battle with the anxiety and managed to gain control.

"You're right," Charity gasped. "I can't run away yet. I have to explain to Brett."

Meredith looked genuinely alarmed now. "Explain what to Brett?"

"That I can't do this. I tried. God knows, I tried. I told myself that it was the right thing to do for everyone. But it's not right. Brett is too nice, he doesn't deserve this."

"Deserve what? Charity, you're not making any sense."

"I've got to tell him. I hope he'll understand."

"Maybe we should go someplace private to discuss this," Meredith said urgently. "How about the ladies' room?"

"I don't think that's necessary." Charity rubbed her

forehead. She could not concentrate. Like a gazelle at the water hole, she kept scanning the bushes, watching for lions. "With any luck, I won't be sick until after I get out of here."

Through sheer force of will, a will that had been tempered in fire when she had assumed the reins of her family's faltering department store chain, Charity fought the panic. She made her way through the crowd toward the bar. It was like walking a gauntlet.

Brett and Davis both turned to her as she emerged from the throng. Davis gave her a brotherly grin of welcome and raised his wineglass in a cheerful toast.

"About time you got here, Charity," he said. "Thought maybe you got held up at the office."

Brett smiled affectionately. "You look terrific, honey. Ready for the big announcement?"

"No," Charity said baldly. She came to a halt in front of him. "Brett, I am very, very sorry, but I can't go through with this."

Brett frowned. "Something wrong?"

"Me. I'm wrong for you. And you're wrong for me. I like you very much. You've been a good friend, and you would have made a fine business partner. But I can't marry you."

Brett blinked. Davis stared at her slack-jawed. Meredith's eyes widened in shock. Charity was dimly aware of the hush that had descended on the nearby guests. Heads turned.

"Oh, lord, this is going to be even worse than I thought," Charity whispered. "I am so sorry. Brett, you're a fine man. You deserve to marry for love and passion, not for friendship or business reasons."

Brett slowly put down his glass. "I don't understand."

"Neither did I until now. Brett, I can't go through with this engagement. It would not be fair to either of us. We don't love each other. We're friends and business associates, but that's not enough. I can't do it. I thought I could, but I can't."

No one said a word. Everyone in the room was now staring at Charity, transfixed. The panic surged through her again.

"Oh, God, I've got to get out of here." She swung around and found Meredith blocking her path. "Get out of the way. Please."

"Charity, this is crazy." Meredith caught hold of her shoulders. "You can't run off like this. How can you not want to marry Brett? He's perfect. Do you hear me? *Perfect.*"

Charity could hardly breathe. She was reeling from the shock of her own actions, but she could not pull back from the brink. A devil's brew of guilt, anger, and fear scalded her insides.

"He's too big." She flung out her hands in a helpless, desperate gesture. "Don't you see? I can't marry him, Meredith. *He's too big.*"

"Are you crazy?" Meredith gave Charity a small shake. "Brett is a wonderful, wonderful man. You're the luckiest woman alive."

"If you think he's so damn wonderful, why don't you marry him yourself?" Horrified at her loss of control, Charity jerked free of her stepsister's grip. She hurtled straight into the crowd.

The stunned onlookers dodged this way and that to clear a path for her. Charity dashed across the Oriental carpet and out through the French doors of the lounge.

She did not pause in the mellow, old-world club lobby. A startled doorman saw her coming and leaped to open the front door for her. She rushed past him and went down the front steps, precariously balanced on her three-inch heels. She was breathless when she reached the sidewalk in front of the club.

It was five minutes after eight on a summer evening. Downtown Seattle was still basking in the late sunlight. She spotted a cab that was just pulling up to the curb.

The rear door of the cab opened. Charity recognized the middle-aged couple who got out. George and Charlotte Trainer. Business acquaintances. Invited guests. Important people.

"Charity?" George Trainer looked at her in surprise. "What's going on?"

"Sorry, I need that cab." Charity pushed past the Trainers and leaped into the backseat. She slammed the door. "Drive."

The cab driver shrugged and pulled away from the curb. "Where to?"

"Anywhere. I don't care. Just drive. Please." From out of nowhere, an image of the open sea flashed through her mind. Freedom. Escape. "No, wait, I know where I want to go. Take me down to the waterfront."

"You got it."

A few minutes later, Charity stood at the end of one of the tourist-oriented piers that jutted out from Seattle's busy waterfront. The breeze off Elliott Bay churned her red silk skirts and filled her lungs. She could breathe freely at last. At least for a while.

She stood there clutching the railing for a long time. When the sun finally sank behind the Olympic Mountains, briefly painting the sky with the color of fire, Charity forced herself to face reality.

She was burned out at the age of twenty-nine.

At a time in life when others were just getting their careers into high gear, she was going down in flames. She had nothing left to give to the family business.

She could not go back to the presidential suite of the Truitt department store chain. She hated the very thought of ever stepping foot into her own office.

Wearily she closed her eyes against the guilt and shame that seized her. It was almost unbearable. For five long years, ever since her mother and stepfather had died in an avalanche while skiing in Switzerland, she had tried to fulfill the demanding responsibilities she had inherited.

She had done her best to salvage her step-siblings' legacy and preserve it for them. But today she had reached the limits of whatever internal resources had brought her this far.

She could not go back to Truitt, the corporation that she had never wanted to run in the first place. She could not go back to Brett Loftus, whose bearlike embrace induced panic.

She had to escape or she would go crazy.

Crazy.

Charity gazed down into the dark waters of the bay and wondered if this was how it felt to be on the edge of what an earlier generation would have called a nervous breakdown.

Prologue: Elias

—❧❧—

> Revenge and deep water have much in common. A man
> may get sucked down into either and drown before he
> understands the true danger.
> —"On the Way of Water," from the journal of Hayden Stone

Elias Winters looked into the face of the man he intended to destroy and saw the truth at last. With a
shock of devastating clarity, he understood that he had
wasted several years of his life plotting a vengeance
that would bring him no satisfaction.

"Well, Winters?" Garrick Keyworth's heavy features congealed with irritation and impatience. "You
demanded this meeting. Said you had something to
discuss concerning my company's business operations
in the Pacific."

"Yes."

"Let's hear it. You may have all day to sit around
and shoot the breeze, but I've got a corporation to
run."

"This won't take long." Elias glanced at the deceptively thin envelope he had brought with him.

Inside the slim white packet was the information that could cripple, perhaps even fatally wound, Keyworth International. The contents represented the culmination of three years of careful planning, endless nights spent studying the host of variables involved, countless hours of cautious maneuvering and manipulation.

Everything was at last in place.

In the next few weeks the big freight-forwarding firm known throughout the Pacific Rim as Keyworth International could be brought to its knees because of the information contained in the envelope. The company would likely never recover from the conflagration Elias was ready to ignite.

Elias had studied his opponent with a trained patience and discipline that had been inculcated in him since his sixteenth year. He knew that Keyworth International was the most important thing in Garrick Keyworth's life.

Keyworth's wife had left him years ago. He had never bothered to remarry. He was estranged from his son, Justin, who was struggling to build a rival freight-handling company here in Seattle. What friends Keyworth had were the type who would disappear the moment they heard that he was in financial trouble. He could not even take satisfaction in his renowned collection of Pacific Islands wood carvings. Elias knew that Keyworth had collected them because of the status they afforded, rather than because of any intrinsic interest they held for him.

The company was Keyworth's sole creation. With the monumental arrogance of an ancient pharaoh, he had built his own version of a modern-day pyramid, a storehouse of treasure on which he sat alone.

But Elias had loosened several of the support stones that sustained the massive weight of the Keyworth pyramid. All he had to do now to ensure that the dark waters of vengeance flowed was to keep the contents of the little envelope secret for a few more weeks.

All he had to do was walk out of Keyworth's office right now. It would be so easy.

"You've got five minutes, Winters. Say what you have to say. I've got a meeting at eleven-thirty." Garrick leaned back against his gray leather executive chair. He toyed with the expensive inlaid pen that he held in one beefy hand.

The hand did not go well with the elegant pen, Elias thought. For that matter, Garrick Keyworth did not go very well with his own office. He clashed with the sophisticated ambience the designer had created.

He was in his mid-fifties, a bulky, burly figure in a hand-tailored suit that could not camouflage the thickness of his neck.

Elias met Garrick's shrewd, predatory gaze. It would be such a simple matter to bring him down, now that every piece on the chessboard was in place.

"I don't need five minutes," Elias said. "One or two should do it."

"What the hell is that supposed to mean? Damn it, Winters, stop wasting my time. The only reason I agreed to see you is because of your reputation."

"You know who I am?"

"Hell, yes." Garrick tossed aside the pen. "You're a major player in the Pacific Rim trade. Everyone here in Seattle who is in the international market knows that. You've got contacts, and you've got the inside track in a lot of places out in the Pacific where no one else can get a toehold. I know you've made a killing consulting for off-shore investors." Garrick squinted slightly. "And word has it that you're also a little weird."

"That pretty well sums up my life." Elias got to his feet. He set the envelope carefully down on top of the polished surface of the wide desk. "Take a look inside. I think you'll find the contents—" He paused, savoring the next word with bleak amusement. "Enlightening."

Without waiting for a response, he turned and walked toward the door. The knowledge that Hayden Stone had been right closed around him like the icy waters of a bottomless lake. Years had been wasted. Years that could never be recovered.

"What is this?" Garrick roared just as Elias reached the door. "What game are you playing? You claimed you had something important that you had to tell me about my Pacific business operations."

"It's all in the envelope."

"Goddamn it, people are right when they say you're strange."

Elias heard the sound of tearing paper. He glanced back over his shoulder and watched as Garrick yanked the five-page document out of the envelope. "There's just one thing I'd like to know."

Garrick ignored him. He scowled at the first page of the report. Anger and bewilderment twisted his broad features. "What do you know about my business relationship with Kroy and Ziller?"

"Everything," Elias said. He knew that Keyworth had not yet realized the import of what he held in his hand, but it wouldn't take him long.

"This is confidential information, by God." Garrick raised his head and regarded Elias with the kind of stare a bull gives a matador. "You have no right to possess information about these contract arrangements."

"Do you remember a man named Austin Winters?" Elias asked softly.

"Austin Winters?" Astonishment and then deep wariness appeared in Garrick's eyes. "I knew an Austin Winters once. That was twenty years ago. Out in the Pacific." His eyes hardened with dawning comprehension. "Don't tell me you're related to him. You can't be."

"I'm his son."

"That's impossible. Austin Winters didn't even have a wife."

"My parents were divorced a couple of years before my father moved to Nihili Island."

"But no one ever said anything about a boy."

The knowledge that his father hadn't even talked about him to his friends and acquaintances was a body blow. With the discipline of long practice, Elias concealed the effects of the direct hit Garrick had unwittingly delivered.

"There was a son. I was sixteen years old when you sabotaged my father's plane. I arrived on Nihili the day after they recovered the wreckage. You had already left the island. It took me a long time to learn the truth."

"You can't blame Austin Winters's death on me." Garrick heaved himself to his feet, his florid face working furiously. "I had nothing to do with the crash."

"You cut the fuel lines, knowing it would take months to get replacement parts from the mainland. You knew that Dad only had one plane and that if he couldn't fly, he wouldn't be able to fulfill his freight contracts. You knew his business would collapse if it was put out of action for several weeks."

"A pack of goddamned lies." A dark flush rose in Garrick's jowly cheeks. "You can't prove any of that."

"I don't have to prove it. I know what happened. Dad's old mechanic saw you leaving the hangar the morning that the problem with the fuel lines was discovered. You wanted to take over my father's new freight contracts, and the easiest way to do it was to make it impossible for him to meet his delivery deadlines."

"Austin should never have taken off that day." Garrick's hands clenched into broad fists. "His own mechanic told him the plane wasn't fit to fly."

"Dad patched up the fuel line and took his chances because he had everything riding on those contracts. He knew he stood to lose his entire business if he failed to make the deliveries. But the fuel line cracked open when the Cessna was a hundred miles from land. My father never had a chance."

"It wasn't my fault, Winters. No one held a gun to Austin's head and made him climb into that old beat-up Cessna that day."

"Have you ever studied the nature of water, Keyworth?"

"What's water got to do with any of this?"

"It's a very unusual substance. Sometimes it's incredibly clear, magnifying everything viewed through it. I am looking through that kind of water now. I can see you sitting on a pyramid built on the ruins of my father's Cessna that lie on the floor of the sea."

Garrick's eyes widened. "You're crazy."

"The broken pieces of the plane are beginning to disintegrate, aren't they? The whole structure will eventually crumble beneath you. And when it does, your pyramid will collapse and you will fall into the sea, just as my father did."

"The rumors are right. You're really out there in the ether, aren't you?"

"But I see now that there's no need for me to rush the process. It will all happen in good time. I wonder why it took me this long to understand that."

Garrick looked torn between fury and incredulity. "I don't have any use for this nonsense. Or for you. Get the hell out of my office, Winters."

"When you read those papers you're holding, Keyworth, you'll realize how close you just came to disaster. I've decided not to sabotage your Pacific operations the way you sabotaged my father's plane. It will be interesting to see what you do with your reprieve. Will you tell yourself that I was weak? That I didn't have the guts to carry out my plans? Or will you look down into the water and see the rot on which you've built your empire?"

"Get out of here before I call security."

Elias let himself out of the plush office and closed the door behind him.

He took the elevator down to the lobby, walked outside, and came to a halt on Fourth Avenue. It was the last week of July, and it was raining in Seattle.

He turned and started down the sidewalk. His reflection watched him from the windows of the street-front shops.

He could see the past clearly through the painfully transparent water that covered it. But the gray seas that hid his own future were murky and opaque. It was possible that there was no longer anything left of value to seek in that uncharted ocean.

But he had to start the search. He no longer had a choice. Today he had finally realized that the alternative was oblivion.

Without conscious thought, he turned at the corner and started walking down Madison Street toward the waterfront. As he gazed out over Elliott Bay, he made a decision.

He would begin his new life by accepting the legacy that Hayden Stone had left to him: a pier known as Crazy Otis Landing and a small curiosity shop called Charms & Virtues, both in the northern part of the state in a little town named Whispering Waters Cove.

1

◦◦◦

Only the most discerning observer can sense the deep, hidden places in the seas of another's life. And only the unwary or the truly brave dare to look into those secret depths.

—"On the Way of Water," from the journal of Hayden Stone

He waited deep in the shadows at the back of the poorly lit shop, a patient spider crouched motionless in his web. There was something about the very stillness emanating from him that made Charity believe he would wait as long as necessary for his prey to venture too close.

"Mr. Winters?" Charity hesitated in the open doorway, clipboard in hand, and peered into the gloom-filled interior of Charms & Virtues.

"Ms. Truitt." Elias Winters's voice came out of the darkness behind the cash register counter. "Please come in. I had a feeling you might show up sooner or later."

He had spoken softly from the far end of the cavernous old wharf warehouse, but Charity heard every word. A tiny tingle of combined interest and alarm went through her. His voice was as deep as the sea, and it beckoned her with the same dangerous allure. She took a cautious step through the doorway and tried to shake off the strange mix of wariness and excitement that gripped her. She was here on business, she reminded herself.

"Sorry to bother you," she said briskly.

"It's not a problem."

"I'm the owner of Whispers, the bookshop at the other end of the pier."

"I know."

An extraordinary quality underlay the very ordinary words. Charity had the feeling that she was being summoned. Uncertainty made her pause.

When in doubt go into full executive mode, she told herself. She had been out of the intense, competitive corporate world for a year, but she could still tap the old skills when she needed them. The important thing was to take charge immediately. She cleared her throat.

"As the President of the Crazy Otis Landing Shopkeepers Association, I want to take this opportunity to welcome you to our little group," she said.

"Thank you."

Elias Winters did not sound particularly impressed. On the other hand, he did not sound unimpressed, either. There was something unnaturally calm about that dark, velvety voice. She wondered if he was tanked to the gills on tranquilizers and then decided that was highly improbable. No one who was stuffed full of sedatives could have managed to infuse so much subtle power into such softly spoken words.

She took a step closer. A floorboard creaked. The gentle lapping of the waves beneath the aging pier was clearly audible in the solemn quiet. Another step produced a ghostly moan from a protesting timber. Dust motes danced in the air.

Whenever she entered Charms & Virtues, she thought of haunted houses and old cemeteries. As she had occasionally pointed out to the previous owner, Hayden Stone, a little dusting and some decent lighting would do wonders for the place.

Elias stood, unmoving, behind the counter. He was cloaked in the false twilight created by the weak lamps and the little slits of windows located high on the walls. She could not make out his face. In fact, she could barely distinguish him from the looming bulk of the antique fortune-telling machine positioned just behind the counter.

Elias Winters had opened the doors of Charms & Virtues three days ago on Monday, the first day of August. Thus far she had caught only brief glimpses of him as he came and went down the central walkway between the pier shops. She had been left with disturbing images that intrigued her and aroused her curiosity.

For some reason she was pleased that he was not too tall, just under six feet. A rather nice height for a man, Charity reflected. He was not built like a side of beef, either. There was, however, a disturbing aura of elegant, lean strength about him. He did not walk, he paced.

Each time she had seen him he had been wearing a dark, long-sleeved pullover and a pair of jeans anchored at the waist by what appeared to be a leather thong. His nearly black hair was a little too long for a man who appeared to be in his mid-thirties.

Yesterday Charity had assigned her counter assistant, Newlin Odell, the task of foisting off Hayden Stone's obnoxious parrot, Crazy Otis, on the new owner of Charms & Virtues. The excuse she had instructed Newlin to give to the unsuspecting Winters was that Crazy Otis missed his old, familiar surroundings. It was true, as far as it went. Otis had fallen into a serious depression when Hayden had failed to return from his last trip to Seattle. It was Charity who had nursed the ungrateful bird through the trauma.

She had held her breath while Newlin ambled down the length of the pier to deliver Crazy Otis and his cage. She had fully expected that Elias would refuse to accept the responsibility. But to her unmitigated relief, Newlin had returned empty-handed.

Newlin's only comment on Elias was that he was "kinda strange." Newlin tended to be a young man of few words. Luckily he could sell books and magazines.

"I'd also like to talk to you about some business matters that concern all of us here on the Landing," Charity continued crisply.

"Would you like a cup of tea?"

"Tea?"

"I just made a pot." Elias set two round, handleless cups on the grimy counter. "A very fine grade of China keemun. The Abberwick Tea & Spice shop in Seattle imports it especially for me."

"I see." Charity did not know any men who drank tea. All the men she knew in Seattle were into espressos and lattes. Here in Whispering Waters Cove, they tended to favor plain coffee. Or at least they had until Bea Hatfield, owner of the café a few doors down on the pier, had installed the town's first espresso machine three months ago. "Yes. Thanks. I'd appreciate a cup."

"Please come back here and join me." The deep voice echoed in the cavelike surroundings.

Feeling uncomfortably like a small, very reckless fly, Charity made her way through the cluttered shop.

Elias seemed to be alone. She glanced around to be
certain, but there definitely were no customers to dis-
turb the tomb-silent atmosphere. She frowned. This
was just the way things had been when Hayden Stone
had run Charms & Virtues.

The curiosity shop had been closed since Hayden's
death two months ago. Hayden had been away in Seattle when he had collapsed from a heart attack. A
quiet funeral had been arranged by some unknown
associate in the city. It had all been over before Charity or any of the other shopkeepers on the Landing
had even learned of their odd landlord's demise.

There was no question but that Hayden would be
missed by the Crazy Otis Landing crowd. He had been
a little strange, but he had also been a sympathetic
landlord.

No one had ever gotten to know him well. Hayden
had lived in his own world, detached and remote from
those around him, but he had never been rude or
unfriendly. Everyone had accepted him as a harmless eccentric.

His death had precipitated a potential financial ca-
tastrophe for the shopkeepers of the pier, however.
The threat had roused Charity's executive instincts,
which had lain dormant for months. Like a butterfly
emerging from a cocoon, she had shaken out her wings
and allowed them to dry in the sun. She was determined to head off disaster before it overtook her new-
found friends.

Her plans required that the shop owners form a
united front. That meant that the new proprietor of
Charms & Virtues had to be convinced to get with
the program.

She went forward determinedly between the aisles
formed by the sagging, disorganized counters. What
little summer sunlight managed to filter into the room

through the high, narrow windows was dimmed by the years of grime on the glass.

Charity wrinkled her nose at the sight of the heavy shroud of dust that covered the assortment of bizarre goods heaped on the display tables. She was dismayed to see that the new proprietor had made no effort to tidy the premises. The goods were still stacked willy-nilly on the counters. There was no organized pattern to the displays.

Odd little carvings were piled high in one corner. A jumble of brass bells and whistles overflowed a nearby packing crate. Small, colorfully dressed dolls with exotic faces painted with startlingly grim expressions tumbled from a box. Plastic masks leered down from the walls. Below was a counter laden with invisible-ink pens, little magic smoke-producing tubes, and puzzles composed of interlocking metal rings.

And so it went throughout the shop. Oddities and imports from far-off lands filled the shelves of Charms & Virtues. Handwoven straw baskets from the Philippines sat next to a hoard of mechanical toy insects manufactured in Hong Kong. Miniature plastic dinosaurs made in Southeast Asia occupied shelf space with rubber worms produced in Mexico. Cheap bracelets, music boxes, imitation military medals, and artificial flowers littered the countertops. Most of it looked as if it had been sitting in the same spot for years.

The wares sold in the dusty import shop could be described in a single word so far as Charity was concerned. And that word was *junk*. The new owner would have to apply some energy and enthusiasm if he wanted to revive his newly purchased small business. She made a mental note to present him a feather duster as a welcome gift. Perhaps he would take the hint.

Charity had never figured out just how Hayden Stone had managed to make a living from Charms & Virtues, or the pier rents, for that matter. He had lived a life of stark simplicity, but even eccentrics had to pay real estate taxes and buy food. She had finally concluded that he'd had a private income from some other source.

"I don't have any milk or sugar," Elias said.

"That's all right," Charity said hastily. "I don't take anything in my tea."

"Neither do I. Good tea should be as clear as a pool of pure water."

The comment brought back memories. "Hayden Stone used to say the same thing."

"Did he?"

"Yes. He was always muttering weird little Zenny comments about water."

"Zenny?"

"You know, Zen-like. He once told me that he was a student of some sort of ancient philosophy that had been forgotten by almost everyone. He said there was only one other person he knew who also studied it."

"Hayden was more than a student. He was a master."

"You knew him?"

"Yes."

"I see." Charity forced herself to a more confident pace. She held her clipboard in front of her as though it were a talisman and summoned up what she hoped was a bright smile. "Well, on to business. I realize that you haven't had a chance to get settled here on the Landing, but unfortunately the lease problem can't wait."

"Lease problem?"

"The shopkeepers have decided to band together as a group to deal with our new landlord, Far Seas,

2 5

Incorporated. We'd like you to join us. We'll have a great deal more negotiating power if we go in as a united front."

Elias lifted a simple brown teapot with a curiously precise but fluid motion. "What do you intend to approach Far Seas about?"

"Renewing our leases." Charity watched, fascinated, as Elias poured tea. "As you no doubt know, this pier was owned, lock, stock, and barrel, by Hayden Stone, the former proprietor of this shop."

"I'm aware of that." A muted shaft of sunshine from one of the ceiling-high windows slanted briefly across the right side of Elias's face. It revealed a bold, hawklike nose and savage cheekbones.

Charity drew a deep breath and tightened her grip on the clipboard. "From what we can gather, at the time of Hayden's death, the ownership of the Landing was transferred automatically to a company called Far Seas, Incorporated."

A low hiss interrupted Charity before she could continue. It was a familiar sound. She spared a brief glance for the large, brilliantly plumed parrot that was perched arrogantly atop a fake tree limb on a stand behind the counter.

"Hello, Otis," Charity said.

Crazy Otis shifted from one clawed foot to the other and lowered his head with a menacing movement. His beady eyes glittered with malice. "Heh, heh, heh."

Elias examined the bird with interest. "I sense some hostility here."

"He always acts like that." Charity made a face. "He knows it irritates me. And after all I've done for him, too. You'd think that bird would show some gratitude."

Otis cackled again.

"I took him in after Hayden died, you know," Charity explained. "He was extremely depressed. Moped around, let his feathers go, lost his appetite. It was terrible. He was in such bad shape I was afraid to leave him alone. During the day he sat on the coatrack in my back room office. I kept his cage in my bedroom at night."

"I'm sure he's grateful," Elias said.

"Hah." Charity glared at the bird. "That bird doesn't know the meaning of the word."

Crazy Otis sidled along the tree limb, muttering with evil glee.

"You don't know how lucky you were, Otis," Charity said. "No one else on the pier was willing to take charge of you. More than a couple of people suggested that we try to sell you to some unsuspecting tourist. And one individual, who shall go unnamed, wanted to call the pound and have you taken away. But I was too softhearted to allow that. I gave you shelter, food, free rides on Yappy's carousel. What did I get in return? Nothing but nasty complaints."

"Heh, heh, heh." Otis flapped his clipped wings.

"Take it easy, Otis." Elias reached out with one long-fingered hand and scratched the bird's head. "An obligation exists until it is repaid. You owe her."

Crazy Otis grumbled, but he stopped chortling. He half-closed his eyes and promptly sank into a contented stupor as Elias stroked his feathers.

"Amazing," Charity said. "The only other person that bird ever treated as an equal was Hayden Stone. Everyone else is just so much old newspaper beneath Crazy Otis's grubby claws."

"Otis and I had a long talk after Newlin brought him over here yesterday," Elias said. "He and I have decided that we can share this shop together."

"That's a relief. To tell you the truth, when I sent Newlin down here with that nasty beast, I expected you to refuse to take him. In all fairness, Crazy Otis isn't your responsibility. Just because you took over Charms & Virtues doesn't mean you have to take charge of him."

Elias gave her a long, considering look. "Otis wasn't your responsibility either, but you took him in and gave him a home for the past two months."

"There wasn't much else I could do. Hayden was very fond of Otis, and I liked Hayden, even if he was a little weird."

"The fact that you liked Hayden didn't mean that you had to take care of Otis."

"Unfortunately, it did." Charity sighed. "Somehow, Crazy Otis has always seemed like one of the family here on the pier. A particularly unpleasant relative, I admit, one I'd prefer to keep stashed out of sight in the attic, but, nevertheless, a relation. And you know what they say about your relations. You can't choose them. You have to take what you get."

"I understand." Elias stopped rubbing Otis's head and picked up the teapot again.

"You don't have to keep him, you know," Charity said in a burst of rash honesty. "He's not a very lovable bird."

"As you said, he's family."

"Parrots like Otis have long life spans. You'll be saddled with him for years."

"I know."

"Okay," Charity said, cheered by the fact that Elias was not going to change his mind on the subject. "Otis is settled. Now about this situation with Far Seas."

"Yes?"

"All of the rents on the pier are due to be renegotiated before the end of September. Today is the fourth of August. We've got to act quickly."

"Just what action do you plan to take?" Elias set down the teapot.

"As I said, we want to approach Far Seas as a united front." Charity realized with a start that she was staring at his hands. They were very interesting hands, powerful hands imbued with a striking, utterly masculine grace.

"A united front?" Elias watched her as she hurriedly raised her gaze from his hands to his face.

"Right. United." She noticed that his eyes were the color of the sea during a storm, a bleak, steel gray. Her fingers clenched around the clipboard. "We intend to contact Far Seas immediately. We want to lock in long-term leases at reasonable rents before the corporation realizes what's happening here in Whispering Waters Cove."

"What is happening here?" Elias's mouth curved faintly. "Aside from the impending arrival of our visitors from outer space?"

"I see you've already met some of the Voyagers?"

"It's a little hard to miss them on the street."

"True." Charity shrugged. "They're quite an embarrassment to the town council. Most of the members think the Voyagers give Whispering Waters Cove a bad image. But like the mayor says, one way or another, the cult should be gone by the middle of August."

"What happens then?"

"Haven't you heard?" Charity grinned. "Gwendolyn Pitt, the leader of the group, has told her followers that the alien spaceships will arrive at midnight on the fifteenth to take them all away on an extended tour of the galaxy. During said tour, everyone will apparently be treated to a lot of pure sex and philosophical enlightenment."

"I've been told it's difficult to mix the two."

29

"Yeah, well, evidently the aliens have mastered the problem. As you can imagine, the town council is hoping that when nothing happens that night, the Voyagers will figure out that the whole thing is a hoax and will leave Whispering Waters Cove bright and early on the morning of the sixteenth."

"In my experience people tend to cling to a belief even when they are confronted with clear evidence that it's false."

"Well, it won't bother me or anyone else here on the pier if some of them decide to stay in the area," Charity admitted. "Most of the Voyagers seem pleasant enough, if a little naive. A few have become good customers. I've made a killing during the past two months with paranormal and New Age titles."

The long blue and white tunics and bright headbands worn by the members of the Voyagers cult had become familiar sights in and around the small town. Gwendolyn Pitt and her followers had arrived early in July. They had parked their motley assortment of trailers, motor homes, and campers on a patch of prime-view land that had once been an old campground.

The town's mayor, Phyllis Dartmoor, had initially been as hostile toward the group as the council members, but after a short flurry of fruitless efforts to force the Voyagers out of town, she had become surprisingly sanguine about the situation. Whenever the local newspaper produced an editorial denouncing the newcomers as a blot on the landscape, she reminded everyone that the cult would likely disintegrate in the middle of August.

"The Voyagers do add some local color," Elias said as he handed Charity one of the small, handleless cups.

"Yes, but they don't enhance the new upscale image that the town is trying to create to draw tourists."

Charity took a sip of tea. The warm liquid rolled across her tongue, bright, subtle, and refreshing. She savored the feel of the brew in her mouth for a few seconds. The man did know his tea, she thought.

"Like it?" Elias watched her intently.

"Very nice," she said as she put the cup back down on the counter. "There is something very distinctive about keemun, isn't there?"

"Yes."

"Well, back to business. Actually, it's the town image thing that makes it necessary for those of us here on the pier to move quickly on the lease issue."

"Go on." Elias sipped tea.

"The mayor and town council would like to see this pier converted into a boutique art mall filled with cutesy shops and antique galleries. They want to attract high-end tenants. But in order to do that, they have to convince the owner of the landing to remove the current shopkeepers. We're not exactly trendy, you see."

Elias glanced around at his own gloom-filled store. "I get the picture. And you think Far Seas will go along with the council's plans to kick us out?"

"Of course. Far Seas is a big corporation in Seattle. Its managers will be interested only in the bottom line. If they think they can lease these shops to a lot of up-market art dealers who can afford sky-high rents, they'll jump at the chance to get rid of us. Or, they may try to sell the landing itself."

"What do you know about Far Seas?"

"Not much," Charity admitted. "Apparently it's some kind of consulting firm involved with the Pacific Rim trade. A couple of weeks ago all of us here on the pier received a letter from Hayden Stone's attorney instructing us to start paying our rents to Far Seas."

"Have you spoken to anyone at Far Seas?"

"Not yet." Charity smiled grimly. "It's a question of strategy."

"Strategy?"

"I decided it would be best to wait until the new owner of Charms & Virtues arrived before we made our move."

Elias took another meditative sip of tea. "So at this point you're operating on a lot of assumptions about Far Seas?"

The hint of criticism irritated her. "I think it's safe to assume that Far Seas will react in the same way that any large company would in this situation. As the new owner of a piece of commercial real estate, the company will naturally want to get the highest possible rate of return. Or the best offer, if it chooses to sell the pier."

"When one studies an opponent's reflection in a pool of water, one should take care to ensure that the water is very, very clear."

Charity eyed him uneasily. "That sounds like more of Hayden Stone's old sayings. Were you a very close friend of his?"

"Yes."

"I suppose that's why you got Charms & Virtues?"

"Yes." Elias's eyes were unreadable. "It was his legacy to me. I also got his cottage."

"I'm sorry to be the one to tell you this, Mr. Winters, but you won't hang on to your legacy for long if we don't get those leases renegotiated with Far Seas. We've got to move fast now that you're here. There's a strong possibility that someone on the town council or Leighton Pitt, a local realtor, will contact Far Seas directly."

"Elias."

"What? Oh, Elias." She hesitated. "Please call me Charity."

"Charity." He repeated her name the way he sipped tea, as if he were tasting it. "Unusual name these days."

"You don't meet a lot of people named Elias, either," she retorted. "Now, then, if you'll just give me a few minutes to explain our plans for dealing with Far Seas, I'm sure you'll see how important it is for you to join with us."

"Yes."

"I beg your pardon?"

Elias raised one shoulder in a lethally graceful movement. "As the new owner of Charms & Virtues, I see the importance of joining with you in your— what did you call it? Ah, yes. Your united front. I've never been part of a united front before. How does it work?"

She smiled with satisfaction. "It's quite simple, really. I'm the president of the shopkeepers association, so I'll do the actual negotiating with Far Seas."

"Have you had much experience with this kind of thing?"

"Yes, as a matter of fact, I have. I was in the corporate world before I moved here to Whispering Waters Cove."

"Charity Truitt." Recognition gleamed in the depths of Elias's eyes. "I thought the name sounded familiar. Would that be the department-store Truitts of Seattle?"

"Yes." Charity's spine stiffened in automatic reflex. "And before you say anything else, let me answer all your questions in three sentences. Yes, I'm the former president of the company. Yes, my stepbrother and stepsister are now running the business. And, yes, I intend to remain here in Whispering Waters Cove."

"I see."

"While I am no longer involved in the operation of

Truitt department stores, I haven't forgotten everything I learned during the years I ran the company. If your résumé is stronger than mine, I'll be glad to turn the job of confronting Far Seas over to you."

"I'm satisfied that you're the best person for the task," he said gently.

Chagrined, Charity set the clipboard down on the counter. "Sorry to sound so belligerent. It's just that my decision to leave Truitt last summer was, uh, complicated and difficult."

"I see."

She studied him closely, but she could not tell if he had heard the rumors of a broken engagement and a nervous breakdown. She concluded that he had not. He showed no signs of curiosity or concern. But, then, he showed no real emotion of any kind, she thought. She decided to plunge ahead.

"The pier is prime property," she said. "We're going to have to fight to keep our shops."

"Something tells me that you will be successful in renegotiating your leases."

"Thanks for the vote of confidence." Charity glanced at Crazy Otis. "If I'm not successful, we're all going to be looking for new locations. And that includes you, Otis."

"Heh, heh, heh." Otis slithered along the perch until he reached the far end. He stepped off the fake branch onto Elias's shoulder.

Charity winced, recalling the occasions when Otis had climbed onto her arm. Elias did not seem to notice the heavy claws sinking into his dark green pullover.

"Another cup of tea?" Elias asked.

"No, thanks." Charity glanced at her watch. "I'm going to call Far Seas this afternoon and see if I can get the lease negotiations started today. Wish me luck."

"I don't believe in luck." He looked thoughtful. "The stream flows inevitably into the river and then on into the sea. The water may take on different aspects at various points in its journey, but it is, nevertheless, the same water."

Newlin was right, Charity thought. Elias Winters was kind of strange. She smiled politely. "Fine. Wish me good karma or something. We're all in this together, remember. If I don't pull this off, everyone on this pier is going to be in trouble."

"You'll pull it off."

"That's the spirit." Charity turned to go. Belatedly she recalled the other item on her agenda. "I almost forgot. The shopkeepers are having a potluck here on the pier Monday night after we close for the day. You're invited, naturally."

"Thank you."

"You'll come?"

"Yes."

"Good. Hayden never came to the potlucks." Charity glanced at the notes on her clipboard. "We still need hot dishes. Can you manage an entrée?"

"As long as no one minds if it doesn't contain meat."

Charity laughed. "I was just about to tell you that a couple of us here on the pier are vegetarians. I think you're going to fit in nicely."

"That would be a novel experience," Elias said.

Charity decided not to ask him to elaborate. Something told her she would not like the answer. Her comment had only been a polite, offhand remark. She doubted that Elias made those kinds of comments. She had the feeling that everything he said was laced with several layers of cryptic meaning. She'd had the same sensation whenever she talked to Hayden Stone. It did not make for a lot of comfortable, casual conversation.

Charity experienced a surge of relief as she walked quickly out of the dark confines of Charms & Virtue into the sunlight. She hurried down the wide corridor between the shops and entered the airy, well-lit premises of Whispers.

Newlin Odell looked up from a bundle of weekly news magazines that he was placing on a rack. His thin features were pinched in the expression of someone who had just recently returned from a funeral. For Newlin, that was normal.

He was a skinny young man of twenty-four. His narrow face was partially obscured by a scruffy goatee and a pair of wire-framed glasses. Charity was almost certain that he trimmed his lanky brown hair himself. It hung in uneven hunks around his ears.

"How'd it go?" Newlin asked in his blunt, economical fashion.

Charity paused in the doorway of her small office, aware of a familiar wave of sympathy for Newlin. She had hired him a month ago when he had shown up out of nowhere to ask for a job. He had come to Whispering Waters Cove to be near his girlfriend, a young woman named Arlene Fenton, who had joined the Voyagers. He spent the time that he was not working at Whispers trying to coax Arlene away from the influence of the cult.

Having thus far failed in his mission to talk sense into Arlene, Newlin had stoically determined to wait out the situation. He hoped that on the fifteenth of August Arlene would finally understand that she had been taken in by a scam.

Charity sincerely hoped that he was right. She found his devotion to Arlene heartwarming and quixotic in an old-fashioned, heroic sense. But she secretly worried about what would happen if Arlene did not come to her senses at midnight that night. Having nursed a depressed parrot for two months, she was not eager to deal with a stricken Newlin Odell.

"You were right, Newlin," Charity said. "Elias Winters is kind of strange. He was a friend of Hayden Stone's, so I guess that explains it. But the good news is that he's willing to go along with the rest of the shopkeepers in order to negotiate the new leases."

"You gonna call Far Seas?"

"Right away. Cross your fingers."

"It's gonna take more than luck to talk Far Seas into giving you a break on the leases if Pitt or the town council has already gotten to 'em and convinced 'em that the pier is valuable real estate."

"Don't be so negative, Newlin. I'm banking on the fact that the town council doesn't yet know who owns Crazy Otis Landing. We only found out ourselves a couple of weeks ago. I told everyone on the pier to keep quiet."

"I don't think anyone's blabbed."

"I hope not." Charity pushed open the door of the back room and wound her way through stacks of boxes to her desk.

She sat down and reached for the phone. Quickly she punched in the number for Far Seas, Inc., which had been included in the letter Hayden Stone's attorney had sent to the shopkeepers.

There were some odd noises on the line, a click, and then the phone finally rang on the other end. Charity wondered if the call had been forwarded. She waited impatiently until the receiver was lifted.

A newly familiar voice answered.

"Charms & Virtues," Elias said.

2

Shallow water sometimes reveals shallow answers. But deep water holds deep questions.

    —"On the Way of Water," from the journal of Hayden Stone

The riptide rush of fate swept through Elias a second time in less than five minutes when Charity stormed back through the front door of Charms & Virtues.

So the strange sense of anticipation that he had experienced the first time he saw her had not been a fluke.

He watched, fascinated, as she bore down on him via an aisle formed by display counters. He had deliberately subjected himself to this second experiment in order to verify the initial results. No question about it. He felt as if he were being swept out into very deep water.

Not good. Not good at all.

But oddly beguiling.

"Who are you, Elias Winters, and what kind of a game are you playing?" Charity demanded.

Elias did not look at his wrist to check the time. He hadn't worn a watch since he was sixteen. But he needed to regain some sense of control. He forced himself to look away from the red fire buried deep in the curving wings of her heavy, dark hair. The battered old cuckoo clock on the wall provided a convenient distraction.

"I'd estimate that took approximately one minute, forty-five seconds, give or take a couple of seconds. You're fast, Ms. Truitt. Very fast. Did you run the whole length of the pier?"

"You timed me?"

Crazy Otis, who was back on his perch nibbling on a large seed, chortled.

"Quiet, Otis," Elias commanded gently.

Otis subsided, but there was a cheerfully malicious gleam in his eyes. He cracked the seed that he gripped in one claw with a particularly loud crunch.

Elias noticed that there was a distinctive gleam in Charity's vivid hazel eyes, too, but it was neither cheerful nor malicious. She was simply outraged.

She was several inches shorter than he was, but she somehow managed to glare at him down the length of her very straight nose. Her full, soft mouth was compressed into an uncompromising line. There was unmistakable warmth just beneath her delicate cheekbones.

Elias felt his insides tighten. He did not understand his own reaction. Something indefinable in her drew his whole attention.

"Mr. Winters—"

"Elias."

"*Mr. Winters*, I want an explanation, and I want it now. You're up to something, that's obvious."

"Is it?"

"Don't you dare start answering questions with questions. That's manipulative, sneaky, and downright passive-aggressive."

"If there's one thing you can be sure of when you deal with me, Charity, it's that when I'm feeling aggressive, there's nothing passive about it."

"You know something? I believe you. That still leaves manipulative and sneaky. And I warn you, *Mr. Winters,* I know everything there is to know about manipulative and sneaky. I grew up in the corporate world."

"I appreciate the warning," Elias said softly.

He liked the way the skirts of her gauzy, white cotton dress billowed and snapped around her gently rounded calves. Only a short while ago when she had arrived to introduce herself, those same skirts had floated discreetly, even protectively about her legs. Now she was angry, and she and her skirts had both thrown discretion to the winds.

The deep sensual hunger rising within him made him uneasy. An attractive, strong-minded woman in a summer dress and strappy little sandals was always an appealing sight, but his reaction today was definitely over the top. What was wrong with him?

Perhaps he shouldn't be too hard on himself, he thought glumly. It had been a long time since he had been involved with a woman. His long-planned vengeance had become an all-consuming passion during the past few months as his grand scheme moved into its final phase. It had become so strong that it had temporarily blotted out even the desire for sex.

And then Hayden Stone had died, and everything had changed forever. Ever since Hayden's death he had felt as if he had been cut adrift on a dark, roiling sea. None of his reactions seemed quite normal. He had lost his sense of internal balance. This intense response to Charity Truitt was a good example.

She was not the sort of woman who normally aroused his interest. For years he had been drawn to the cool types found in film noir movies. Savvy, sophisticated women who wore a lot of black. Women who moved in the high-stakes world of the Pacific Rim trade, either as power brokers or as powers behind thrones. Some had been attracted to him because of the contacts and connections he could offer. Some had simply wanted the satisfaction of being seen with a man who was as powerful as themselves. Others had been intrigued by the perception of danger. Whatever the terms of the sexual bargain, Elias had always made certain that the exchange of favors had been equal.

But Charity was different. He sensed intuitively that if he pursued the relationship, there would be no simple, straightforward arrangement with her. She would be demanding and difficult in ways that he had always avoided.

"Are you or are you not connected to Far Seas?" Charity fumed.

Elias flattened his hands on the glass counter in front of him. "I am Far Seas."

"Is this a joke?"

"No." He considered briefly. "I don't think I know any jokes."

"Well? Where's the rest of the company?"

"The rest of it?"

She threw up her hands. "Secretaries, clerks, managers, and assorted flunkies."

"My secretary took another job a few months ago. I didn't bother to replace her. There are no clerks or managers, and I never could get any reliable flunkies."

"That is not funny."

"I told you, I don't do jokes."

"Assuming you're telling me the truth, why were you so secretive about the fact that you now own the pier?"

"I learned a long time ago never to initiate a business discussion. The clear spring waters of open dealing and plain-speaking are too often mistaken as evidence of weakness. I was taught to let others come to me."

Charity came to a halt in front of the counter. "You mean you prefer to hold the advantage. I get the point. But for the record, I never took any of those expensive seminars from rip-off management consultants on how to do business according to the principles of the Tao. I prefer to do business the old-fashioned way. Level with me, Winters. Do you really own Crazy Otis Landing?"

"Yes." Elias looked into her huge hazel eyes and wondered at the deep wariness he saw beneath the anger. He recalled vague gossip about the chaos that had followed a failed merger between Truitt and a company called Loftus Athletic Gear. There had been an abrupt resignation of Truitt's CEO. Rumors of a problem with said CEO's nerves. He had paid little attention because neither Truitt nor Loftus were involved in Pacific Rim trade.

"Well?"

"Hayden Stone did not leave only Charms & Virtues to me," Elias said. "He left me the whole pier."

"Plus the cottage on the bluff." She narrowed her eyes. "That's a lot of real estate. Why would he leave so much to you?"

Elias chose his words carefully. "I told you, Hayden was my friend and my teacher. He helped me establish Far Seas."

"I see. Just what kind of company is Far Seas?"

"A consulting firm."

Charity crossed her arms beneath her breasts. "What kind of consulting?"

"I provide contacts, connections, and advice for business people who deal in Rim trade." He probably should have made that past tense, he thought. He wondered if he would ever again return to his former line of work. For some reason, he doubted it. Along with everything else in his life these days, it seemed to be drifting farther and farther away from him.

"Whispering Waters Cove is not exactly a thriving outpost of Pacific Rim business."

He smiled slightly. "No, it's not."

"So what are you doing here?"

"You're a very suspicious woman, Charity."

"I think I have reason to be suspicious under the circumstances. A short while ago, I made the mistake of assuming that you were one of us here on the pier and that we would all be going up against Far Seas together."

"I warned you that when one studies an opponent's reflection in a pool of water, one should take care to ensure that the water is very, very clear."

"Yeah, yeah, I heard you the first time. Forget the double-talk. When I want philosophy, I'll go to Ted."

"Ted?"

"Ted Jenner. He has that little shop called Ted's Instant Philosophy T-Shirts next to the carousel. You must have seen it."

Elias recalled the racks of T-shirts billowing in the breeze at the end of the pier. The shirts all bore various legends and slogans that ranged from the clever to the crude. "I've noticed it."

"I should hope so. You walk by it every day. The

least you could do, by the way, is drop in and introduce yourself to your fellow shopkeepers."

"I've just met you," he pointed out.

She raised her eyes toward the ceiling in an expression of acute disgust. "Never mind. Let's get back to more pressing issues. What's your excuse for failing to tell me the truth about yourself while I was explaining the lease situation here at the pier?"

"You never asked."

She threw up her hands. "How was I supposed to know that you were Far Seas?"

"The degree of clarity of the water makes no difference if one does not ask the right questions about the image that is reflected on the surface."

She gave him a fulminating look. "Skip the mumbo-jumbo and get to the point. If you are who you say you are, then tell me the truth. What do you intend to do about the pier leases?"

"Renew them at the present rates when they come due in September."

Charity's mouth fell open, revealing neat, small white teeth. She closed it swiftly. "Why would you do that now that I've told you about the town council's plans to use Crazy Otis Landing as the centerpiece for the new, improved Whispering Waters Cove?"

"I don't know."

"I beg your pardon?"

Elias shrugged. "I don't have an answer to your question. That's one of the reasons I came here to Whispering Waters Cove. To get some answers."

To get a clear answer, a man had to ask a clear question. And he was not able to do that. Every time he looked into the water to see his own true face, he caught only glimpses of a badly distorted reflection.

Elias rolled smoothly out of the last of the series of

ancient exercises Hayden Stone had taught him. The deceptively effortless movements formed a pattern known as Tal Kek Chara. They represented the physical expression of the ancient philosophy in which Hayden had been a master. Tal Kek Chara was a state in which mind and body were balanced in a flow of energy for which water was a metaphor.

The coiled length of leather anchored to Elias's wrist represented the philosophy, and it was named for it. Tal Kek Chara was a weapon as well as a way of living.

As Elias ended the pattern, the leather thong unfurled as if it were an extension of his arm. It whipped around the branch of a nearby tree with enough force to chain the limb but not enough to snap it in two. Control was everything in Tal Kek Chara.

Elias straightened and retrieved the supple strip of leather. He took a few seconds to assess the effects of the routine he had just completed. He was breathing deeply but not hard. The light breeze off the waters of the cove was already drying the perspiration on his bare shoulders. It had been a solid workout, but he had not exhausted himself. That was as it should be. Excess in anything, including exercise, was a violation of the basic principle of Tal Kek Chara.

Automatically, he snugged the leather back into place around his waist. He wore it outside the loops of his jeans. A weapon that could not be accessed in a hurry was useless.

He turned and walked back along the cliff toward the spare little cottage that Hayden Stone had lived in during the last three years of his life. When he reached the garden gate he opened it and stepped into the serene, miniature landscape Hayden had created. The focal point of the garden was a calm reflecting pool.

Elias went up the porch steps and opened the front door of his new home. He paused, as Hayden had taught him, to allow his senses to absorb the essence of the small dwelling. All was well.

He padded barefoot across the hardwood floor. There were no chairs in Hayden Stone's house. There wasn't much else in the way of furniture, either. Two cushions, a low table, and a sisal mat completed the living room decor. A wide, clear, heavy glass dish that was partially filled with water sat in the center of the table. The walls were bare.

The only touch of color in the room was Crazy Otis. It was enough. The parrot's brilliant plumage was spectacular against the simple surroundings.

Otis, perched on top of his open cage, bobbed his head in greeting and stretched his wings.

"I'm going to take a shower, and then I'll fix us both some dinner, Otis."

"Heh, heh, heh."

Elias went into the single bedroom, which contained only a futon-style bed and a low, heavily carved wooden chest. The kitchen and bath were outfitted with the basic necessities of modern life, but basic was the operative word.

Bicoastal interior designers and architects talked effusively about minimalist design, but Hayden Stone had created the real thing here in this small, spare house. Its simple lines held layers of complexity that only one skilled in the ways of Tal Kek Chara could detect.

Elias's house in Seattle had been similar to this one. It had been located on the edge of Lake Washington. He had sold it shortly after the interview with Garrick Keyworth. He did not miss it. Tal Kek Chara had taught him not to become too attached to things. Or to people. Since his sixteenth year, Hayden had been the one exception. And now Hayden was gone.

Elias went into the bathroom, stripped off his jeans, and stepped into the stall shower. Memories of Hayden flickered in his mind. For some reason he saw a scene from his sixteenth year, a scene that had occurred several months after his father had died.

"Why do we have to sit on the floor when we eat our meals?" Elias asked as he folded his legs on the cushion in front of the low table.

"To remind us that we don't need chairs." Hayden ate soba noodles with a strange, handmade implement that was part fork, part knife. It was both a sophisticated eating utensil and an equally useful weapon. "A man who learns that he can be comfortable without a chair will learn that he can be comfortable without a lot of other things, as well."

"Did they teach you that in that monastery where you stayed after you got shot up?"

"Among other things."

Elias knew the story well. Hayden had been a mercenary until his thirty-fifth year, a man of violence who had sold his unique talents and pieces of his soul to anyone with the money to pay the price. In a world where small brushfire conflicts simmered in many regions of the globe, there was never a lack of buyers for the commodities that Hayden offered for sale.

He had been badly wounded in the course of one such campaign, a small civil war that had been waged in a forgotten corner of the Pacific. He had been left for dead by his companions.

Hayden had told Elias that he had fully expected to die there in the jungle. Not relishing the prospect of being gnawed on by some of the local wildlife while still alive, he'd readied a bullet for himself. He'd figured that he had just enough strength left to pull the trigger one last time.

But he kept making excuses for putting off the inevitable.

Hayden had told himself he would wait until nightfall or until the pain became unbearable or until the first hungry scavenger appeared. His instinct for survival had been stronger than he had expected, however. Night came, the pain got worse, and he could hear the tell-tale rustle in the bushes. But still he could not bring himself to put a bullet in his brain. Something stilled his hand.

The monks found him shortly after dawn.

"How long were you at the monastery?" Elias asked as he fiddled with his noodles. He was getting the hang of the eating tool, but he still fumbled a bit with it.

"I lived in the House of Tal Kek Chara for five years. Now the House lives inside me." Hayden deftly dipped noodles into a clear broth and transferred them to his mouth. He chewed in silence for a while. "You did well in your training this afternoon."

"It felt better. Smoother, somehow." Elias plunged noodles into his own bowl. He grimaced when broth splattered on the table. Until he had come to live with Hayden, he'd been addicted to hamburgers and pizza. Now the thought of eating meat made him queasy for some reason. "Do you think I'll ever be as good at Tal Kek Chara as you are?"

"Yes. Better, probably. You've started your training at a younger age than I did, and your body responds well to the discipline. You have a natural talent, I think. And it helps that you're not walking around with an old bullet in your gut."

Elias stared at him. Hayden made few references to

his former life as a professional mercenary. "Yeah, I guess so."

"But learning the exercises of Tal Kek Chara will not teach you what you need to know in order to be able to look into the pool and see truths."

"If this is going to be another lecture on the subject of giving up my plans to get Dad's killer, you might as well forget it, Hayden. Someday I'm going to find out who sabotaged the Cessna. And when I do, I'll make sure the bastard pays."

"A man cannot see truth clearly in water that is clouded with strong emotions. One day you will have to decide whether revenge is more important to you than owning your own soul."

"I don't see why I can't have my revenge and still own my own soul."

Hayden looked at him with ancient eyes. "I have great faith in you, Elias. You're smart, and you have power. You will eventually see clearly enough to find your true inner flow."

He had finally seen the truth about revenge, Elias thought as he toweled off and reached for a clean shirt and a pair of jeans. But he could not yet see the truth about himself.

He went into the kitchen to prepare his dinner. The routine brought back more memories of Hayden. This time he gently pushed them aside and lost himself in the creative process of cooking.

Half an hour later he sat down on a cushion in front of the table. He surveyed the bowl of steamed rice, seaweed-flavored soup, and vegetable curry and realized that, for the first time in a long while, some part of him was not plotting vengeance or business strategy. No, for the first time since the funeral, he had a new goal.

He wanted to go to bed with Charity Truitt.

"It won't be simple or easy, Otis. I have a gut feeling that Charity is one of those very expensive women Hayden used to warn me about. He said that to lure one, a man had to be prepared to pay a very high price."

"Heh, heh, heh."

He'd have to get her attention with something costly, Elias thought. A piece of himself, no doubt.

An expectant hush fell on the small crowd gathered at the end of the pier just as Charity set her herbed couscous and green lentil salad down on the picnic table. She tried without any success to squelch the tingle of anticipation that went through her. She didn't need the low, speculative mutters of those around her to know who had arrived.

If someone hadn't chanced to look in his direction, though, no one would have heard Elias approach. His low, soft, well-worn boots made no sound on the pier timber. When he moved through the shadowed areas created by the walls of the various shops, it was difficult to make out his gliding form.

Charity was intrigued by the sight of a covered bowl in his hands. His eyes met hers as if he had been waiting for her to notice him. He inclined his head a scarce fraction of an inch in greeting. Charity heard a small gasp. She was chagrined to realize that the person sucking in air in such an inelegant manner was none other than herself.

"There he is," Radiance Barker whispered in her high, sweet, breathy tones.

Radiance, who in a former life had been named Rhonda, cultivated the feathery voice. It went with the rest of her, which Charity privately thought of as neo-hippie. Much to Radiance's everlasting regret, she was too young to have been a genuine flower child of the fabled sixties. She considered herself a spiritual descendent of the era, however, and dressed accordingly. Long loops of beads decorated the flowing, multipatterned dress she wore this evening. Her waist-length hair was trimmed with a flower-studded headband.

"Something fishy about this whole thing, if you ask me," Roy Yapton, better known as Yappy, declared. "Hayden Stone was weird, but at least he played straight with us. I ain't so sure about this guy."

"He owns the whole shooting match," Bea Hatfield said, "so you'd best watch what you say, you old coot."

Roy and Bea were both on the far side of sixty. They'd been operating their respective pier enterprises for over twenty years. Their affair had been going on for as long as anyone could recall. No one knew why they had never married or why they bothered to pretend that they were just good friends.

"Wonder what he brought to eat." Ted Jenner absently scratched his stomach, which was barely concealed by an extra-extra-large T-shirt. "I'm starving."

The shirt was from his own shop, Ted's Instant Philosophy T-Shirts. Charity glanced at the slogan on the one he was modeling this afternoon. It read, *I May Be Dysfunctional, But You Are Definitely Crazy*.

"That's not exactly news." Radiance scanned Ted's portly figure with an amused expression. "You're always starving. I keep telling you that if you switched to vegetarian, you'd lose weight."

"Dropping a few pounds ain't worth havin' to eat nothin' but nuts and berries for the rest of my life," Ted said cheerfully. "Even if Charity can cook that bunny rabbit food better than anyone I ever met."

It was a long-running argument. No one paid much

attention. Everyone was too busy watching Elias, and no one seemed quite certain how to greet him. Last week he had been one of them, albeit a newcomer, Charity thought. This week he was their landlord.

The new leases had not yet been signed. Elias had nearly two months to change his mind about extending the old contracts, and everyone present knew it.

Charity decided that, as president of the shopkeepers association, it was her duty to take charge. She smiled very brightly at Elias when he reached the little group.

"You can put your dish down on that table over there," she said, deliberately infusing her voice with authority. It was an old trick, one she'd had to learn quickly when she'd faced a roomful of creditors all bent on salvaging what they could from the failing Truitt department store chain. It was her intuition that had gotten her through those early days of overwhelming responsibility. She would use it to deal with Elias. "Have you met everyone?"

Elias glanced around as he set the covered pan down next to Bea's potato salad. "No."

Charity hastily ran through the introductions. "Roy Yapton. He owns the carousel. Bea Hatfield. She owns the Whispering Waters café. Radiance Barker, owner of Nails by Radiance. Ted Jenner. He operates the T-shirt shop. And you've already met Newlin Odell. Newlin works for me."

"Hi." Newlin peered at Elias through his small, round glasses. "Otis doing okay?"

"He's fine." Elias nodded politely at the small circle of faces. Then he leaned back against the pier railing, crossed one booted foot over the other, and folded his arms.

Charity lifted her chin and prepared to pin him down. "I've explained to the other shopkeepers that you've committed to renew the leases at the old rates."

Elias nodded, as if the subject held little interest.

Yappy scowled. "That true, Winters?"

"Yes," Elias said quietly.

"Whew." Bea fanned herself with a napkin. "I don't mind telling you, it's a relief to hear you say it. Charity told us that you know all about the town council's plans to turn Whispering Waters Cove into a sort of Northwest Carmel."

Elias glanced out over the cove, his gaze thoughtful. "Somehow, I don't see that happening."

Ted frowned. "Don't be too sure about that. Phyllis Dartmoor, our illustrious mayor, says the council's already come up with a couple of possible new names for Crazy Otis Landing. They want something that sounds more up-market, she says. Indigo Landing or Sunset Landing."

Charity groaned. "They sound so generic. No character at all."

"Charity has been doing battle with Mayor Dartmoor and the council on a regular basis since the spring," Radiance told Elias. "We all go to the monthly council meetings, but we let Charity do the talking. She's good at that kind of thing."

"I see." Elias rested his gaze on Charity. "Crazy Otis Landing suits the pier. I don't see any reason to change it."

"I'm glad you agree with the rest of us," Charity said. "But I warn you, you're going to get a lot of pressure to change not only the name of the pier but everything else about it as well."

"I think I can handle it," Elias said softly.

Charity was not sure how to deal with that simple statement. She looked around at the others. "Well, what do you say we eat first and then talk business?"

"Good idea," Ted said. "What did you bring, Winters?"

"Chilled green-tea noodles with a peanut dipping sauce," Elias said. "There's some wasabi on the side for those who like it hot."

Charity stared at him in astonishment.

"Figures," Ted muttered. "Another fancy gourmet vegetarian from Seattle. May have to put a ban on you folks moving here to the cove. You're ruining our regional cuisine."

Radiance raised her brows. "You mean those old hallowed recipes such as hamburger casserole and mushroom soup gravy are in danger of going extinct? Groovy."

Bea laughed. "Better look to your laurels, Charity."

Radiance giggled. "Charity is a fantastic cook," she explained to Elias. "Ted grumbles a lot, but even he likes her food."

"Best bunny food in the Northwest," Ted agreed as he ambled over to the picnic table.

"You can say that again." Yappy crossed to the table and removed the cover from Elias's dish. He smiled with satisfaction at the sight of the green noodles. "But I think we may have some real serious competition here, folks."

Charity heard the universal relief in the good-natured laughter that followed Yappy's comment. She felt the tension seep out of the group as everyone trooped toward the buffet table.

A few minutes later she sat down on a bench, a plate of Elias's green noodle concoction in her hand. The late summer twilight settled softly over the cove. The last rays of the setting sun turned the sky to molten gold.

Elias sat down near Charity. She glanced covertly at his plate and noticed that it was laden with her couscous and lentil salad. For some obscure reason, that pleased her.

The sound of chanting voices drifted across the cove. It was accompanied by the lilting tones of a badly played flute and the throb of a drum.

"What the hell is that?" Elias asked.

"The Voyagers," Radiance answered. "They chant the sun down every evening. You probably can't hear them from your house on the bluff, but the prevailing wind sometimes carries the sound across the cove to the pier."

"Bunch of crazies," Ted said around a mouthful of green noodles.

Radiance frowned. "I think it's a lovely ancient custom."

Elias glanced at her. "Ancient custom?"

"They used to do things like that in the old days," Radiance said.

Elias paused, a forkful of Charity's salad halfway to his mouth. "Which old days?"

Charity hid a grin.

Radiance softened her voice to a level approaching reverence. "The sixties."

"Ah." Elias nodded very soberly. "Those old days."

He caught Charity's gaze and gave her a slow, deliberate wink. She almost dropped her fork.

"Be interesting to see how long the Voyagers keep up the quaint custom after winter hits," Yappy said gruffly. "They'll freeze their asses off out there on the beach if they try that in November."

"They won't be here in November," Bea reminded him. "Like the mayor says, they'll all leave when the spaceships fail to show up as promised."

Newlin Odell raised his head abruptly. His eyes glittered with anger behind the round lenses of his wire-rimmed glasses. "That chanting-down-the-sun shit is just another stupid ritual Gwendolyn Pitt created to add a little color to her scam."

"Take it easy, Newlin," Ted advised. "So far as anyone can figure out, Pitt ain't doing anything illegal. Believe me, if there was something shady going on with the Voyagers, the town council would jump on it. They'd send the police chief out there in a red-hot minute if they had grounds."

"That's true," Yappy agreed. "Council's been looking for an excuse to get rid of the Voyagers ever since they arrived. I'm surprised Leighton Pitt isn't more upset than he is. You'd think he'd be real pissed. He owns half-interest in that old campground the Voyagers are using."

Elias ate couscous with a contemplative air. "Is there a connection between Leighton Pitt, the realtor, and Gwendolyn Pitt, the cult leader? Or is the name just a coincidence?"

"No coincidence," Bea said. "Leighton is the wealthiest man in town. Gwen is his ex-wife. They both used to run Pitt Realty together. But Leighton divorced Gwen a year ago to marry a new real estate agent named Jennifer who went to work for them. It was a real nasty mess."

Elias flicked an inquiring glance at Charity. "And Pitt's ex-wife showed up this summer with the spaceship cult in tow?"

"Uh-huh." Charity swallowed another spoonful of delicious noodles. "Makes you wonder, doesn't it?"

"Gwen's up to something, all right," Yappy said thoughtfully. "Must be cash in it somewhere. That woman always knew how to make money. Pitt was an idiot to dump her. Business hasn't been near as good for him since the divorce. Jennifer can't sell real estate the way Gwen could."

"I'll tell you one thing." Newlin's fingers clenched

around his can of pop with such force that the thin aluminum crumpled. "Gwendolyn Pitt shouldn't be allowed to get away with what she's doing. She's ruining people's lives. My Arlene turned over every cent she had to that damn cult. Someone oughta take care of Gwendolyn Pitt for good."

3

~~~~~

The most dangerous tides are those that swirl in the
shallow waters close to shore where a man believes himself
to be safe.

      —"On the Way of Water," from the journal of Hayden Stone

"Things are looking up, Davis. The new owner says
he's going to renew the leases."

Charity scrunched the phone between her ear and
her left shoulder so that she could use both hands to
unpack a box of books that had just been delivered
that morning. Although she had no competition as yet
from other bookstores, she believed in getting the latest titles out onto the shelves as quickly as possible.
Regardless of the size of a business, good service was
the best way to ensure customer loyalty. She had sal-
vaged the Truitt chain with that simple philosophy and
saw no reason to alter it with Whispers.

"You got contracts yet?" Davis asked with typical
pragmatism.

"No. And you don't have to tell me that nothing is for sure until the paperwork is signed in September, but this guy is a little off-beat. Definitely not your typical business mentality. I think we may be out of the woods."

"He knows about the town's plans for Crazy Otis Landing, and he still wants to renew the leases at the old rates?" Davis still sounded skeptical.

"That's what he says." Charity smiled as she discovered twenty copies of the latest Elizabeth Lowell release in the box she had just opened. She had a long waiting list of readers who were eagerly awaiting the popular author's newest title.

"What kind of an idiot did you get for a landlord, Charity? Must be a life-is-like-a-box-of-chocolates kind of guy."

"Not exactly. He's more of a noodle type."

"Noodle? As in limp?"

Charity grinned in spite of herself. "Wrong image, Davis. Try a life-is-like-water-but-if-the-water-is-muddy-you-don't-get-a-good-reflection kind of guy."

"That doesn't sound like much of an improvement."

"Actually, he's a little hard to explain." After ten days of having Elias in the vicinity, Charity found him more intriguing than ever. Her curiosity and her fascination were both growing daily. "Anyway, about the leases. As I told you, we're not in the clear yet. But you know me and my intuition. Something tells me that Winters isn't likely to change his mind next month."

"The new owner's name is Winters?" Davis asked sharply.

"That's right. Elias Winters."

"I'll be damned." Davis whistled softly. "There wouldn't be any connection to Elias Winters of Far Seas, Inc., would there?"

"Yes. You know him?"

"Not personally." Davis paused. "But I've heard about him. Very low-profile, very high-impact. Has important connections all over the Rim. Knows the right people."

"He said something about being a consultant."

"Word has it that if you need help establishing business relationships in certain quarters, he can open doors. For a price. He can also close them, if you get my drift."

"I see. How come I've never heard of him?"

"He's strictly Pacific Rim, and Truitt wasn't involved in Rim trade when you were at the helm. But lately Meredith and I have been thinking about expanding again. Winters's name came up when I started exploring certain possibilities."

"Hmm."

"Far Seas is apparently a one-man operation," Davis continued. "Winters seems to have carved out a unique niche for himself. He handles business negotiations in small, out-of-the-way places that others ignore. Speaks two or three obscure languages that no one else can be bothered to learn. His clients are usually very rich and very low-profile. The kind of big-money movers and shakers who avoid the spotlight. Are you sure you're dealing with *that* Elias Winters?"

"That's who he claims to be. What's wrong?"

"I'm not sure," Davis admitted. "But I can tell you that, from what I've heard about him, he sure as hell isn't the type to move to a small town and run a curio shop on a pier. Keep your eyes open, Charity. My guess is he knows something you don't."

"Such as?"

"Who can tell? Maybe one of his off-shore clients is preparing to move into Whispering Waters Cove."

"And Elias is here to pave the way?"

"It's about the only scenario I can think of that fits the situation. If that's the case, there's money involved. A lot of it."

"He said he inherited the pier from Hayden Stone, our former landlord."

"Maybe he did and maybe he didn't," Davis mused.

"Are you saying that Elias Winters may have bought the pier from Hayden Stone on behalf of his off-shore client?" It worried Charity that she had not thought of that possibility herself. She hoped that she hadn't been out of the corporate world for so long that she could no longer trust her instincts. "Maybe that's why Hayden was in Seattle when he had the heart attack. He was finalizing the deal. But why would Elias lie about it?"

"Use your head, Charity," Davis said. "The pier may be just the beginning. If Winters has been hired to pick up a lot of choice real estate for a foreign investor, the last thing he'll want to do is drive up property values around Whispering Waters Cove."

"True." Charity drummed her fingers on the stack of Elizabeth Lowell books. "If he's going to buy a lot of land here, he'll try to keep the purchases quiet as long as possible. Pretending that he inherited the pier and has no immediate plans for it would be one way of deflecting curiosity."

Davis chuckled. "You told me the town council wants to go boutique. But, believe me, they ain't seen nothin' yet. Not if Winters is a player. Some of his clients are into world-class resort developments. Waterfront is perfect for them."

Charity considered the situation. The town council was already salivating at the prospect of converting Crazy Otis Landing into an upscale tourist attraction. But the mayor and the council members would go wild if they believed that a wealthy off-shore investor was preparing to turn Whispering Waters Cove into a glitzy destination resort.

"Any company moving into Whispering Waters Cove will want to pick up the land it needs as cheaply as possible before word gets out and all the locals decide to try to make a killing," Davis added. "It's common to send in a good point man to buy the big parcels before anyone knows what's happening."

Crazy Otis Landing was a nice chunk of waterfront property, Charity reflected. It could easily form the heart of a major resort. "You think Elias Winters might be acting as a point man for an off-shore investor?"

"I think it's a reasonable assumption, given what I've heard about Winters."

"But why would he agree to renew the leases at the old rates if he wanted the pier for his client?" Charity was irritated by the rising note in her own voice. There was no call to get emotional about this, she thought. This was business. She had once been very good at business.

"If I'm right, you're looking at three- to five-year planning in action," Davis explained.

"In which case, renewing the leases for another year is no big deal," Charity said glumly. "Whoever is behind the operation may not intend to start construction for another couple of years."

"Exactly. Why not let the present tenants hang around for a while? Besides, it helps maintain the low profile."

"I get the picture," Charity said. "If we want secure leases here on the pier, we'd better negotiate them for at least three years, maybe five."

"Relax," Davis said cheerfully. "It's not your problem. You've got more than enough business savvy to keep your little bookstore going regardless of what happens to the pier. In fact, a major resort would probably do wonders for your bottom line. People on vacation read a lot. You'll be okay."

But Bea, Yappy, Radiance, and Ted didn't have her skills and business acumen, Charity thought. They were not what anyone in the corporate world would call players. It was true that they had improved their business methods in the past year, but their little shops were unlikely to survive a sudden, major redevelopment of the pier.

"Thanks, Davis. Say hello to Meredith."

"I will. About time you came into the city to see us, isn't it?"

"I'll get in one of these days."

"Good." Davis hesitated. "Sure you're not bored with running that little pier shop yet?"

"I'm sure."

"I have a bet with Meredith. I give you six more months before you come back to Seattle."

"You're going to lose, Davis."

"We'll see. By the way, Charity, one more thing."

"Yes?"

"A word of warning. Watch your step with Winters. Rumor has it he's not just a player, he's a winner. Every time."

"No one wins every time, Davis."

Charity said good-bye and hung up the phone. For a while she gazed blindly at the display of mystery titles that occupied a large section of one wall.

Why was she feeling such a letdown, she wondered. She knew how the players in the business world worked. Davis had only said aloud things that she, herself, should have suspected from the start.

The truth was that she did not want to believe that Elias Winters might be deliberately deceiving her. During the past ten days she had begun to hope that he was exactly what he claimed to be. A man who had come to Whispering Waters Cove to find some answers.

A man who had something in common with her.

The soft knock on the kitchen screen door came after dinner that evening. It startled Charity, who was sitting at the table, filling out yet another in the seemingly endless series of bureaucratic forms that always threatened to drown a small business. Her pen slipped on the first letter of her name just as she was about to add her signature. The *C* came out as an odd little squiggle.

Charity threw down the pen and shot to her feet. She whirled to face the door. A dark figure loomed on the step.

"Who's there?"

"Sorry, didn't mean to scare you." Elias gazed at her through the screen. His eyes gleamed in the fading twilight.

The small jolt of fear dissolved into a tingle of relief. "You didn't scare me. I just didn't hear you." Feeling like a fool for having overreacted, she rose and went to the door. "I had a little trouble here last month. Someone trashed my house one evening while I was out attending a meeting of the town council. I guess I'm still a little jumpy."

"I didn't know Whispering Waters Cove had a crime problem."

"We don't. At least, not by city standards. The police chief, Hank Tybern, suspects some summer visitors. But there's no way to prove it. I just hope they've left the area. What are you doing here? Is something wrong?"

"No. I was out for a walk. Thought I'd stop by and

see if you'd care to join me for an evening of scintillating theatrical entertainment."

"Entertainment? What entertainment?" The temptation to open the screen door was almost overwhelming.

"A musical drama known as chanting down the sun. I can arrange front-row seats for tonight's performance if you're interested."

Charity smiled in spite of herself. "It's gotten lousy reviews."

Elias shrugged. "I figure it beats trying to conduct a conversation with Crazy Otis. He wanted to go to sleep."

"So you got bored and decided to come over here?" The minute the words were out of her mouth, she wished she could recall them.

"It was just a thought." Elias held up a hand. His expression was shadowed and unreadable. "If you'd rather do paperwork . . ."

She winced. "Hang on, I'll get my key."

He contemplated her kitchen table and chairs as she turned away from the door. "Bet you didn't buy this stuff down at Seth's New & Used Furniture Mart, did you?"

Charity flicked a glance at the sleek lines of her expensive Euro-style furnishings. "Nope. Brought it with me from Seattle. Thank God the vandals contented themselves with throwing food from the refrigerator onto the floor and writing nasty words on the walls. They didn't get around to ruining my furniture."

With the key in the pocket of her jeans and the door securely locked behind her, she joined Elias in the warm summer twilight. Without a word they walked toward the old dirt path that wound along the bluffs above the beach.

Charity had made it a habit to walk several times a

week. It was part of the self-prescribed therapy she had adopted to help herself recover from burnout. She hadn't had a panic attack in months, unless one counted the brief twinge she had gotten when Rick Swinton had tried to pressure her into a date.

The storms of anxiety had eased shortly after she had moved to Whispering Waters Cove. But she had maintained the exercise ritual along with some of the other stress-reducing techniques she had learned. They had become her talismans.

She loved the feel of the cove breeze on her face. It never failed to invigorate all her senses and clarify her mind. Tonight the effect was even stronger than usual. She was keenly aware of Elias gliding along beside her. She sensed the heat and the quiet strength in him even though he had not touched her.

"I'm sorry I snapped at you a few minutes ago," she said at last. "The crack about your coming over to see me because you were bored was rude."

"Forget it."

She hesitated and then decided to take the plunge. "I had an interesting conversation with my brother today."

There was just enough light to reveal the brief, wryly amused twist of Elias's mouth. "I assume that I was the main topic of conversation."

She sighed. "To be honest, yes. Davis said he'd heard of you and Far Seas, but he'd never met you."

"I've heard of him, too. Our paths have never crossed."

"He said I should be cautious around you, that you weren't the type to run a little curio shop on a small-town pier. He said you were probably here in Whispering Waters Cove on behalf of some big off-shore client."

Elias kept his gaze on the grove of trees that

marched down to the edge of the bluff. "My reasons for being here have nothing to do with business. Your brother's assumptions are based on a faulty premise."

"In other words, he's looking through murky water?"

"Sounds like you picked up a few things from Hayden."

Charity smiled briefly. "I liked Hayden. But I never felt as if I knew him well. There was always something distant and remote about him. It was as if he existed in his own private universe."

"You're right. He did. As far as I know, I was the only one he ever allowed into that universe."

Something buried in his dark voice caught and held Charity's attention. "He was more than a friend to you, wasn't he? And more than a teacher, too."

"Yes."

She breathed out slowly. Empathy washed away several layers of common sense and caution. "It's only been two months since his death. You must miss him."

Elias was silent for a couple of heartbeats. "I was with him when he died. Made him go to the emergency room. He kept telling me it was a waste of time, that he was going to die and that no doctor could do anything about it. But he knew that he had to let me take him to the hospital because if I didn't, I would have spent the rest of my life wondering if he could have been saved. He would have preferred to die quietly in my house."

"But you took him to the emergency room, and he died there, instead?"

"Yes." Elias looked out over the cove. "He was very calm at the end. Centered. Balanced. He died as he had lived. The last thing he said to me was that he had given me the tools to free myself. It was up to me to use them."

"Free yourself from what?"

Another beat of silence. "The need for revenge."

Charity stared at him. "Against whom?"

"It's a long story."

"I don't mind listening."

Elias did not respond for several minutes. Charity began to think he had no intention of answering her question. But after a while, he finally began to talk.

"My parents were divorced when I was ten. I lived with my mother. She . . . suffered from bouts of depression. One month after I turned sixteen, she took her own life."

"Oh, God, Elias. I'm sorry."

"I went to live with my grandparents. They never recovered from their grief. I think they always blamed my father for my mother's problems. And some of that blame shifted to me after her death. I waited for my father to send for me. I never heard from him."

Charity's throat tightened. "Where was he?"

"He ran a small air-freight business based on an island named Nihili."

Charity frowned. "I've never heard of it."

"Few people have. It's out in the Pacific. After a while I talked my grandfather into paying my way out to Nihili. It wasn't hard."

"What happened to your father?"

"Dad had a rival, a man named Garrick Keyworth."

Charity said nothing when he paused again. She simply waited.

"Keyworth sabotaged Dad's only plane. My father knew it, but he took off, anyway. The plane went down out over the ocean."

Charity was stunned. Whatever she had been expecting, it wasn't a tale of murder. "If that's the truth, then it seems to me that you had every right to want revenge against this Keyworth."

"It's not as simple as it sounds. Things rarely are. Dad knew the plane had fuel line problems that day, but he chose to take the chance and fly. He had contracts to fulfill. One of the things I never wanted to admit to myself was that he made his own decision to risk his life."

A flash of intuition went through Charity. "He not only risked his own life, he risked leaving you alone, didn't he?"

"You could say that." Elias's smile contained no humor. "Hayden certainly said it a few times."

"Your father may have been guilty of poor judgment, but if you ask me, that still doesn't absolve this Garrick Keyworth. Not by a long shot."

"No, it doesn't. To make a long story short, I arrived on Nihili a couple of days after Dad had gone down. It was Hayden who met me at the airstrip. For reasons of his own, reasons I never fully understood, he accepted me as his personal responsibility. He finished the task of raising me. Helped me start my business. Taught me how to be a man. I owe him more than I can ever repay."

Charity swallowed to keep herself from bursting into tears. "I see. What about the man who sabotaged your father's plane?"

"It took me a long time to learn his identity. After I found out who he was, I spent years devising a way to bring down his empire. And then Hayden died."

"And that changed things?"

"Everything. I looked at Keyworth's reflection in a different light after I said good-bye to Hayden. One of the things I hadn't seen before was that Keyworth has paid a price for his crime. He knows that everything he has today is founded on that one act of destruction. It's eating at his soul. It's what drives him, and it will ultimately destroy him. It's already cost him more than he even knows. I decided to leave him to the prison he's built for himself."

Charity exhaled deeply. "That's a very philosophical way of looking at it. Downright metaphysical, in fact. No offense, but I find it a little hard to believe that you just walked away from that situation and left Keyworth to the great wheel of cosmic justice."

Elias's dark brows rose. "Very perceptive of you. You're right. I wasn't exactly a saint about the whole thing. I went to see Keyworth before I came here. Showed him some documents that proved beyond a doubt that I had the contacts and connections to cripple, possibly even destroy, his operations in the Pacific. *Then* I walked away."

Charity was speechless for a few seconds. "And left him to live with the knowledge that you had had him in your power and let him go?"

"I decided I owed myself that much, at least."

She drew a deep breath. "Very subtle. Perhaps too subtle. Keyworth may think you backed off simply because you were too weak to go through with your plans. Or because you lost your nerve."

"I doubt it," Elias said quietly. "I studied him for a long time before I made my move. I know him well."

"You think that the knowledge that he was vulnerable to you will add to the pressure that's building inside him?"

"Perhaps." Elias made a small, dismissing movement with his hand. "Perhaps not. It doesn't matter. Keyworth no longer concerns me."

"Yet you spent years plotting against him?"

"It takes time to set up the kind of vengeance I planned."

Charity held her breeze-tossed hair out of her eyes. "Did you have the confrontation with Keyworth shortly before you moved here?"

"Yes."

"Whew. You've been through a lot during the past couple of months, haven't you? The death of your friend Hayden, the showdown with Keyworth, a major career shift, and a move to a new location."

He glanced at her with a curious expression. "What's that supposed to mean?"

"Just that you'd score pretty high right now if you were to take one of those psych tests that measures recent stressful events in your life."

"I don't plan to take any psych tests."

"No, I don't suppose you do." For some reason the thought of Elias sitting down to a battery of psychological tests almost made her smile. "You'll probably just gaze into a nice, clear pool of water instead."

"It works for me."

She gave him a sidelong look. "Mind if I ask you a question?"

He appeared to brace himself. "No."

"Why did you tell me all this? On the first day we met I got the distinct impression that you were the strong, silent type."

He smiled. "Still suspicious of me?"

"I prefer to think of it as cautious. Suspicious has paranoid connotations, and I don't think I'm that far over the edge."

"All right. Cautious. The answer to your question is that I gave you a piece of my privacy as a gift because I want something from you in exchange."

"Damn it, I *knew* it." And he had known just how to get past her defenses, she thought furiously.

She was not hurt or even disappointed, she told herself. She had known there would be a catch to this little evening stroll. Elias wasn't the kind of man who would share intimate secrets with anyone unless he had an ulterior motive.

"Let's hear it," she snapped. "What do you want from me? If this has something to do with the lease negotiations, you're wasting your time."

"I don't care about the lease arrangements. All I want from you is the chance to get to know you."

She came to a sudden halt and swung around to face him. "I beg your pardon?"

"You heard me." As if it were the most natural thing in the world, as if they shared a regular habit of walking along the bluffs in the evening, Elias reached out and took her hand. "My turn to ask you a question."

4

~~~

The approaching storm turns the surface of the sea to steel
and silver. Only danger reflects clearly from such a mirror.

　　　—"On the Way of Water," from the journal of Hayden Stone

Charity instinctively tensed as Elias's powerful hand
wrapped around her fingers. He was strong. Stronger
than she had realized. But she still did not sense so
much as a tiny frisson of the old claustrophobic sensation that had seized her during the days when she had
dated Brett Loftus. And certainly nothing of the
twinge of the fight-or-flight response she had felt last
month when Rick Swinton, Gwendolyn Pitt's assistant
cult manager, had attempted to sweep her off her feet
with his oily charm.

At least she now knew for certain that she was
not going to be stuck for the rest of her life with
panic attacks every time a man touched her. What
a relief.

Euphoria shot through her. *Cured at last.* She felt a ridiculous grin curve her mouth.

And then she became aware of an eerie thrill curling through her insides. The sensation was not one of sharp, terrifying anxiety, but it certainly did not have a calming effect.

It took her a moment to recognize the devastating sweep of raw desire. She stopped grinning, caught her breath, and nearly stumbled when she realized exactly what it was that was affecting her senses. So this was how real sexual attraction felt.

"Are you okay?" Elias asked as he steadied her.

"Yes." Damn. She was actually breathless. "Yes, I'm fine. Tripped over a little stone. Hard to see clearly at this time of night. It'll be full dark soon."

He gave her an odd look but said nothing.

She'd had one or two pleasant, sincere relationships over the years, no more than a couple because there had never been any time. Her life had not been her own since the day the avalanche had killed her mother and stepfather. Saving Truitt for the next generation had been her only focus. Then she had developed that stupid phobia to poor Brett.

What with one thing and another, she had never experienced anything even remotely akin to this wild, fluttering excitement.

Please don't let this be another kind of precursor to an anxiety attack, she thought. Please. Not with this man. No more dumb phobias. This feels too good.

What shook her was the sense of intimacy involved. It was as if Elias was allowing her to sample some of his own personal energy. She wondered if he was getting a few tingles from her. Then she wondered what it would be like to kiss him.

Different, she decided after due consideration. Very different. About as out-of-the-ordinary, say, as the arrival of a fleet of spaceships carrying aliens from outer space.

"All right, it's your turn," she said briskly. "What's your question?"

"Hayden mentioned once that when you opened your bookshop a year ago, you single-handedly revived the rest of the businesses on Crazy Otis Landing."

Charity made a face. "That's a gross exaggeration. Tourism has been gradually increasing here in the cove for a couple of years. We've been discovered in a small way, and the pier is a natural draw. All that was necessary was to provide a reason for visitors and locals to stop. A bookstore does that nicely."

"He also told me that under your influence, the other shopkeepers have become more businesslike this past year. He said they come to you for advice. He credited you with convincing Bea to install an espresso machine, for example."

"I had the advantage of having spent several years in the corporate world," she reminded him. "I wasn't cut out for it, but I certainly learned a few things. When the others come to me with questions, I try to help. But the truth is, I owe them far more than they owe me."

"How's that?"

She hesitated, just as he had earlier, searching for the right words. "When I first came to the cove, I was completely burned out." She slanted a quick glance at his profile. "You probably heard a few of the rumors?"

"A few."

She exhaled deeply. "Well, most of them were true. I did make an incredibly embarrassing scene on the night I was to become engaged to a very nice man named Brett Loftus. Had a panic attack, in fact. Right there in front of half the movers and shakers of Seattle. I felt terrible. I mean, it wasn't Brett's fault that he was too big and that I didn't . . . well, never mind."

"Too big?" Elias's voice was oddly neutral.

"Yes, you know." Charity waved a hand in a vague gesture. "Too tall. Too large. All over. For me, that is." That wasn't fair, she thought. Her therapist had explained that Brett's size hadn't been the real problem. Unfortunately, her brain had linked her fear of the relationship with his physical stature. The result had become a full-blown phobia.

"I see." Elias's tone sounded even more strange.

"Have you ever met him?"

"No. But I've seen him. I heard him speak once at a luncheon at one of my clients' business clubs."

"I'm sure that he would be just fine for another woman," she said hastily. "My stepsister, for instance. Lots of women admire, uh, size in a man."

"I've heard that."

"But every time poor Brett . . . well, you know. I just couldn't stand it. He was such a gentleman. He attributed my problems to stress. It was really very awkward."

"Sure. Awkward."

"But the bottom line was that when it came right down to it, the thought of . . . of . . ." She felt herself blush furiously and was profoundly grateful for the deepening shadows. "Doing it. On a regular basis, that is. The way one would in marriage . . . I mean, a man as big as that, well, it was just too much."

"I think I get the picture."

She cleared her throat. "At any rate, the merger I had planned for months did not go through."

"You stepped down from the helm of Truitt department stores."

"Yes. With no warning to my stepbrother and stepsister. I just abandoned them. I spent a few weeks getting therapy, realized I could never go back to the business world, and decided to move. I more or less threw a dart at a map of Washington. And here I am."

"What happened next?"

"A funny thing." Charity smiled. "I rested. Walked a lot here along the bluffs. Got back into cooking. And then one day I went looking for something to read and realized that Whispering Waters Cove had no bookshop. I went down to the pier and talked it over with Hayden. He rented space to me. Within a couple of months I started to feel reasonably normal again."

"You know," Elias said thoughtfully, "under your management, Whispers would flourish in a boutique version of Whispering Waters Cove. You have nothing to fear and everything to gain if the town council's plans work out."

"I'm doing fine as it is. I prefer slow, steady growth. Big leaps are hazardous in business. If you crash, you go down in flames. Besides, my aspirations aren't as high as they used to be. I like small business. I think it's a calling. You get to know your customers personally. There's something very satisfying about it."

"But there's no reason to tie the future of your business to that of the other businesses on the pier," Elias insisted. "Why are you doing it? Why form the shopkeepers association? Why do battle with the mayor and the town council?"

Charity frowned, puzzled by his line of inquiry. "The other shopkeepers are my friends. They welcomed me with open arms when I first came to Whispering Waters Cove. They were generous and supportive, and they've been good neighbors."

"So in order to pay them back, you've committed

yourself to helping them hang on to Crazy Otis Landing?"

"It was the least I could do. You've met them. None of them are what you'd call sophisticated businesspeople. A big corporation would roll right over them."

"True," Elias admitted.

"They all ended up on the pier because there was nowhere else for them to go. They've formed a community. They need each other. I think Hayden understood that."

Elias smiled wryly. "Hayden had no interest in going boutique, himself."

"All I want to do is give the pier shopkeepers a chance to stay where they are as the town begins to pull in more visitors and tourists."

"Do you think that Yappy and Ted and the rest can learn to compete with a bunch of art galleries?"

"If necessary." Charity shrugged. "But who knows? Maybe the upscale shops will never materialize."

"In the meanwhile, you've thrown in your lot with the pier crowd."

She studied him with a long, considering glance. "So have you. If you're telling me the truth about Far Seas' intentions, that is."

The sound of an off-key flute and loud voices rising and falling in an enthusiastic chant forestalled whatever response Elias might have made to her deliberate challenge.

"Looks like the show has started," he said as they emerged from the trees.

Charity looked around. They had reached the outskirts of the old campground. A large assortment of recreational vehicles were clustered together on the bluff overlooking the cove. Several of the vehicles had been decorated with designs that vaguely resembled ancient Egyptian motifs. Others were painted with imaginative futuristic landscapes and bizarre visions of the universe.

There was no one in sight. Gwendolyn Pitt's followers were all down on the beach.

At some point in the distant past, a long fence had been installed along the edge of the bluffs. It stretched the length of the campground. There were two openings, one in the center and one at the far end. Each provided access to a narrow path that led down to the rocky beach.

The droning chant filled the air. Charity looked over the edge of the sagging fence and saw the Voyagers gathered below at the water's edge. There were about twenty of them, she estimated. The number had grown during the past week. There was just enough light left to make out the flowing blue and white robes and the brightly beaded headbands that comprised the cult's uniform.

She saw that the small crowd had formed a circle and linked hands. They swayed to the beat of the drum and flute.

The last of the coppery twilight glow disappeared as the sun sank out of sight behind the mountains. The first star appeared. The chants grew louder. The drum beat faster.

A dynamic figure broke free of the circle and raised her arms above her head in a commanding gesture. Silence fell. The Voyagers turned to face her with murmurs of anticipation.

"That's Gwendolyn Pitt," Charity said to Elias.

"I know. She introduced herself the other day at the grocery store."

"Did she? I've talked to her a few times during the past month. She seems committed to her concept, but I can't quite bring myself to buy into her act. Something about seeing a successful, hard-nosed realtor turn into space alien guru is a little tough to swallow."

"You can say that again." Elias studied the woman on the beach with a thoughtful expression. "Looks like she shops at the same places Radiance Barker does."

He was right, Charity decided. Gwendolyn Pitt looked as if she could have stepped straight out of one of the sixties' era posters Radiance had used to decorate the nail salon.

When she raised her arms, the sleeves of Gwendolyn's gown fell back to reveal rows of wide metal bracelets. But there was still the hint of the professional real estate saleswoman about her in her short, tailored, artificially blond hair and expensive shoes. It did not take much imagination to picture Gwen Pitt in a crisp business suit with a briefcase in hand.

She was in her late forties, not especially attractive, but her features were strong and assertive. There was a certain steely quality about her. Whatever else she was, she was a driven woman. Charity could almost see the sparks.

"Five nights, my friends," Gwendolyn intoned in a loud, sonorous voice that carried up the side of the bluff. "Only five more nights until the great starships come. Midnight of the appointed day will soon be here, and *they* will arrive in all their brilliant splendor."

"Something tells me that woman knows how to close a deal," Elias said.

"Enlightenment awaits, my friends," Gwendolyn continued in rolling accents. "Unparalleled knowledge of our own true sexuality and an understanding of the philosophical laws of the universe shall be ours. Our bodies will be made perfect by advanced alien science. Our lifespans will be vastly extended in order that we may have the time to learn all that we are destined to discover."

The crowd sent up a rousing shout of agreement.

"That is one angry lady," Elias said softly.

Charity glanced at him curiously. "How do you know that?"

"It takes a lot of rage to pull together an operation the size of this scam."

Charity recalled what he had just finished telling her about his own plans to destroy an old enemy. Elias knew whereof he spoke, she thought. She would do well to bear that in mind. The sizzling sexual attraction she was feeling was certainly interesting, but that was no excuse for being stupid where this man was concerned.

"Maybe she really is simply deluded," Charity mused. "I suppose it's possible that she actually believes that the spaceships will arrive."

Elias studied the scene on the beach. "If you're prepared to buy that, I've got a nice pier I can sell you. No, she's not crazy, she's got an agenda. Be interesting to know what it is."

"Power?"

"That's probably part of it, but not the whole. If she just wanted to run a cult for the sake of exercising power, she wouldn't have announced such a close deadline for the arrival of the spaceships."

"I wondered about that myself," Charity said. "The Voyagers just got here last month, and the fifteenth of August is only five days away. She's bound to lose a lot of credibility when the ships don't show."

Elias braced a booted foot on the bottom rung of the fence. He kept his grip on Charity's hand. "There must be some significance to the deadline."

"Most people think she's in it for the money. Newlin says that his girlfriend, Arlene, and the others have turned over their life savings to her."

"That's standard procedure for this kind of thing. But why bring her followers to Whispering Waters Cove? The place has got to hold some bad memories."

"And humiliation." Charity grew thoughtful. "The new Mrs. Pitt is here, after all. Gwen and Jennifer must run into each other at the grocery store and at the post office. A little awkward, to say the least."

"How's Gwen's ex, the real estate broker, dealing with it?"

"Are you kidding?" Charity made a face. "I'm sure Leighton is thoroughly embarrassed by the situation, but he can't force her to leave. She does own half-interest in this campground, after all. He's trying to ignore her."

"And the second Mrs. Pitt? What's her response?"

"I don't really know Jennifer very well. No one does. She's from California."

Elias grinned briefly. "That explains a lot."

"From what I've seen, she's keeping her cool about the whole thing," Charity said. "I guess she figures all she has to do is wait it out until the fifteenth. But it can't be easy for her, either."

"Nothing like having the first Mrs. Pitt running a cult on the edge of town while the second Mrs. Pitt tries to establish herself as the new wife of one of the most influential men in the area."

"True."

"Were you here at the time of the divorce?"

Charity shook her head. "The scandal broke shortly before I arrived. But I know most of the juicy details, thanks to Radiance."

"What's Radiance got to do with any of this?"

Charity chuckled. "She does the second Mrs. Pitt's nails. She's actually grateful to her because Jennifer did a lot to help make fancy acrylic nails fashionable here in town. Until Jennifer showed up with her long, perfect, California red nails, everyone else just used nail clippers."

"How scandalous was the divorce?"

Charity regarded him with speculation. "You know, you don't look like the type to be interested in sordid gossip."

"I collect information," Elias said softly. "Sort of a hobby."

"Hmm, well, according to Radiance, the whole thing blew up one day early last summer when Gwendolyn showed the old Rossiter place to some clients. They all walked into the cottage, which is located in a very isolated location near the point, and found Jennifer and Leighton in bed together."

"Not a pretty picture."

"No. Radiance told me that Leighton and Jennifer had been using the Rossiter place for their rendezvous for several weeks before they were discovered."

"Rough way for Gwen to learn that her husband was cheating on her," Elias said.

"Yes. You can imagine how the gossip flared up again when Gwen and her Voyagers arrived in town last month."

Elias looked down at the beach and watched as Gwendolyn held forth on the exciting events that would take place on the fifteenth. "Something tells me that the fuel that runs Gwendolyn Pitt's engine comes from something more than old-fashioned power and greed."

Charity was suddenly acutely aware of the swift fall of night. The shadows were lengthening around the looming motor homes and campers. "What else besides power and money could motivate her to go to all this effort?"

Elias shifted his enigmatic gaze from the scene on the beach to Charity's face. "You have to ask me that after what I just told you about my plans for Garrick Keyworth?"

"Vengeance? But that doesn't make any sense. How could all this"—Charity spread her free arm out to indicate the Voyagers and their campground—"be about vengeance?"

"I don't know. I'm only saying that there are other motives in the world besides power and money."

The cove breeze shifted. It tugged at Charity's shirtsleeves. She pushed a tendril of hair out of her eyes. "Maybe we'll get the answers on the morning after the spaceships fail to show."

"Maybe." Elias's enigmatic gaze rested on her face.

"There's one thing I'm certain of," Charity continued.

"What's that?"

She wrinkled her nose in disgust. "Gwen Pitt's motives might be obscure, but her sleazy right-hand man, Rick Swinton, is very obvious. He's in this for the money. I'd stake Whispers on it."

"I haven't run into Swinton yet."

"You haven't missed anything." Charity shuddered. "A real creep."

Elias eyed her. "That sounds personal."

"It is. He made a pass at me shortly after the Voyagers got here. The cove is not exactly a mecca for singles, but I wasn't desperate enough to go out with him. When I declined his invitation, he told me I'd be sorry."

Elias grew still. "He threatened you?"

"Not exactly. Just said I'd regret turning him down." Charity smiled. "Believe me, I didn't."

"I'll keep an eye out for him." Elias's hand tightened on hers. "In the meantime, I've got another very important question."

The dark velvet of his voice sent more little chills of excitement down her spine. "What's that?"

"I've been wondering," he said very softly, "how your mouth tastes."

She stared at him. "I beg your pardon?"

"I've been thinking about it for the past ten days." He pulled her gently, inexorably, closer.

She met his eyes, saw the controlled desire in him, and was nearly overwhelmed by the sense of inevitability that descended on her. She knew then that she had been waiting for this ever since he had knocked on her door earlier that evening.

Again she stiffened, instinctively searching for the smallest sign of the heightened anxiety that presaged a panic episode. But all she felt was the rush of sensual anticipation.

Elias was definitely the right size.

He kept one foot on the lowest rung of the fence railing as he drew her forward. A delicious shock went through her when she found herself standing in the intimate space created between his thighs.

The background murmur of the light cove surf and Gwendolyn Pitt's exhortations to her followers faded into the distance. Charity dimly realized that her senses simply could not focus on all the normal stimuli that surrounded her. They were fully engaged with the feel of Elias's hard, lean body against hers. She could feel the heat of him. It drew her with the power of a magic spell.

She reminded herself that just because Elias had confided in her didn't mean that she could trust him. She couldn't even be certain that he had told her the truth. He was a subtle, clever man. Moreover, there was no doubt but that he was a little weird.

Davis's warnings echoed in her brain. *Watch your step with Winters. Rumor has it he's not just a player, he's a winner. Every time.*

But Elias's touch did not trigger any warnings from her nervous system. On the contrary, the closer she got, the closer she wanted to be.

When he lowered his head to take her mouth, she learned in one shattering second that everything she had suspected was true. Kissing Elias was definitely a different experience. Hot, sexy, and incredibly satisfying.

A spectacular flower that had been dormant within her all of her life suddenly blossomed. Elias's muscled thigh tightened against her hip, trapping her between his legs. She put her arms around his neck and parted her lips.

Elias groaned. A shudder went through him.

Charity was enthralled by the sensations that poured through her. Elias's kiss was darker and more mysterious than the fall of night. It was full of arcane secrets and layers of unfathomable meanings. It would take a lifetime to explore this kiss. Joy and excitement soared within her as she sank into the unplumbed depths.

"Damn." Elias tore his mouth from hers with an abrupt, wrenching movement of his head. He sucked in a deep breath.

Charity gazed up at him, astonished. His eyes glittered in the shadows. His expression was grim. His breathing was harsh and ragged, as if he had just run a marathon.

"Sorry," he muttered. "This is happening too fast. I didn't intend it to be like this. Not so soon. Didn't want to rush you."

"It's okay, really." She touched the side of his cheek and felt his jaw clench in response. An invigorating sense of her own feminine power rose within her. "I don't mind in the least."

Elias looked bemused, almost dazed. He stared down at her for a long time and then, with another smothered groan, he covered her mouth once more.

He did what Charity would have sworn was impossible: He deepened the kiss. His arms tightened around her in an urgent move that settled her hips more snugly against his fierce erection. He slid one hand to her ribs and moved it slowly upward until his thumb rested just beneath the weight of one breast.

It was Charity's turn to shudder.

Somewhere in the distance, she heard the chanting resume down on the beach, but she paid no attention. The only thing that mattered in that moment was Elias. His palm moved again, closing over her breast. She could feel the heat of his hand through the fabric of her shirt.

The first muffled shouts barely registered on her awareness. She tuned them out without realizing it until Elias suddenly broke off the drugging kiss.

"What the hell?" He raised his head, listening.

Charity blinked, trying to clear her mind. She felt the sexual tension in Elias transmute into another, equally primitive kind of readiness.

Disoriented, she started to step back.

Another cry sounded.

This time Charity heard it clearly. A woman's voice, half angry, half fearful. "Get your hands off me. I'll tell her. I swear, I will!"

"It came from back there," Elias said. "On the far side of the rest rooms, I think."

He released Charity and spun around in a single, lithe movement. He moved off with an easy, ground-eating stride that took him between a row of aging campers.

Charity saw that he was heading toward a maroon and white motor home parked toward the rear of the campground.

"Let me go, damn you! I'll tell Gwendolyn."

Charity broke into a run and flew after Elias.

By the time she caught up with him, he was vaulting up the steps of the maroon and white motor home. She watched as he yanked open the metal door and exploded through it into the interior.

She heard a startled scream from inside the big vehicle. It was followed by an angry, masculine shout.

"What the hell are you doing?" a man squawked. "Take your goddamned hands off me or I'll have you arrested."

Charity came to an abrupt halt as a figure stumbled wildly through the open door of the motor home. She recognized Rick Swinton immediately.

He wasn't nearly as handsome as usual, she reflected with a sense of satisfaction. In fact, he looked quite silly standing there, flailing about on the top step.

Rick missed his footing and fell. He landed on the ground with an audible grunt.

Elias appeared in the doorway. He was as serene and unruffled as the eye of a hurricane.

Charity surveyed him anxiously. "Are you all right?"

Elias glanced at her as if surprised by the question. "Yes. This jerk was manhandling a woman inside."

"Shit." Rick spit dirt out of his mouth and heaved himself to a sitting position. He shoved curling brown hair out of his eyes and glowered furiously at Elias. "I'm going to have you arrested, you bastard. You hear me, you sonofabitch? I'm gonna sue you for this."

"Going to be a little tough to file a lawsuit and get

a judgment before the spaceships arrive on Monday."
Elias came slowly down the steps. "But you're welcome to try."

A young, attractive woman came to stand in the
doorway. She clutched the lapels of her Voyager robe.

"Arlene." Charity stared, astonished. "Good grief.
Are you okay?"

"Yeah, I'm okay." In the dim glow of a weak campground light Arlene appeared flushed and angry. Her
sandy brown hair had come free of her headband and
stood out in wild disarray around her shoulders. She
glared at Rick as she straightened the folds of her long
hooded, white robe. "Don't you touch me again, Rick
Swinton. Do you hear me? Not ever again."

"Did he hurt you?" Charity hurried toward the
motor home steps.

"He's a nasty little liar, but he didn't hurt me."
Arlene blinked. "What are you doing here, Charity?"

"Elias and I were just out for an evening stroll, and
we heard you shouting."

Rick heaved himself to his feet and brushed the seat
of his black designer chinos. His Voyager blue silk
shirt, which he wore open down to the navel, was also
covered with dust. The multitude of gold chains that
he wore around his neck glinted in the dim light. He
gave Charity a sullen glare. "Should have minded your
own damn business. Not everyone has your problem
with sex. Some of us are normal."

Elias glanced at Charity as he went down the steps.
"You two know each other?"

"Meet Rick Swinton," Charity said. "Gwen Pitt's
assistant."

Elias surveyed Rick with cold disdain. "Let's skip
the handshake, Swinton, I might be tempted to break
your arm."

Rick narrowed his eyes. "You'll be sorry, whoever you are."

"The name is Winters. Elias Winters. Be sure you spell it right when you file your complaint."

"S.O.B."

"This is Arlene Fenton," Charity put her arm lightly around Arlene's shoulders. "She's Newlin's friend."

Elias nodded.

"Oh, my God, Newlin." Arlene's chin came up sharply. Her eyes grew very round. "Charity, promise me you won't tell him about this. It'll only upset him something fierce. You know it will. He's already having a real bad time with the idea of me going off on the ships."

"What, exactly, happened here?" Charity asked.

"Rick told me he had some special information about what's going to happen when the ships come," Arlene whispered. "He told me that I had been chosen as one of the vanguard who would make initial contact. He said he was going to teach me the secret code we'll use to communicate with the aliens."

"Bullshit." Rick gave her a fulminating look. "She came on to me, same as every other bitch under the age of sixty in this burg. When I took her up on the offer, she suddenly turned all righteous. Little cock tease, that's all she is. Just like you, Ms. Tightass Truitt. You're both the kind that gets a man worked up and then yells rape when he tries to get a sample of what they're offering."

"One more word," Elias said softly, "and you won't be in any condition to ask for more samples from any female."

Arlene flung back her head. "You're lying, Rick Swinton. I've been preparing myself for the Journey, just like Gwendolyn told us to do. We're all supposed to be getting ready to move to a higher plane where sex will be a pure, nonphysical experience."

"Give me a break," Swinton muttered.

"And what's more," Arlene shot back, "if I was going to fool around, it wouldn't be with you. I've got me a fine boyfriend, and I'm going to make sure he comes with me when it's time to go aboard the ships. And I'll tell you something else, if Gwendolyn knew how you acted when her back was turned, she'd send you packing."

"Goddamned little bitch." Rick backed up hurriedly when Elias moved in the shadows. "Keep your hands off me, Winters."

"Oh, let him be," Arlene said with acute disgust. "I'm all right, and you can bet I won't let him get me alone again. He's perverted, if you ask me. You should see what he's got inside his motor home. And he thinks it's sexy. Well, I can tell you none of it will matter after next Monday night."

"You can say that again." Rick swung around and stalked off down a dark corridor formed by several campers and some motor homes.

Charity gave Arlene a small hug. "Are you sure you're okay?"

"I'm fine." Arlene heaved a deep sigh. "Rick's a sneaky little twerp who uses his position as Gwendolyn's assistant to try to get it on with every female Voyager in sight. First time he's ever tried anything with me, though."

Elias stirred. "You said that if Gwendolyn knew about his behavior, she'd get rid of him. If that's the case, why don't you tell her?"

"The thing is, she's got so much on her mind right now." Arlene looked uneasy. "Most of us only see her at the evening sundown chant. She spends the rest of her time in her motor home preparing for Monday night. Rick's the only one who's allowed to interrupt her when she's meditating or pursuing her studies."

"I could get her attention for you," Elias offered. "No problem."

"I don't want to cause her any trouble," Arlene said quickly. "Rick Swinton isn't important. He's such a turkey, I wouldn't be surprised if he gets left behind when the aliens come."

"Don't worry," Elias said. "Something tells me that Swinton won't be going on board any starship at midnight on the fifteenth. And neither will anyone else."

Arlene straightened her shoulders with grave dignity. "I can see that you're a nonbeliever. But you and all the others will learn the truth for yourselves. I just wish I could get Newlin to understand. I can't bear the thought of leaving him behind."

Charity patted her shoulder. "Newlin cares about you, Arlene. If things don't work out, remember that he'll be here waiting for you."

Tears glistened in Arlene's eyes. She wiped them away with the back of her hand. "But I want him to come with me to see the galaxy. If he stays behind, he'll be dead and turned to dust by the time I get back."

Elias looked at her. "Sometimes the surface of the water is so distorted by a passing storm that you can't see any truth in it."

Arlene blinked away a few more tears and stared at him uncomprehendingly. "Huh?"

Charity gave her another little hug. "Don't worry about it, Arlene. Elias can be a little obscure. It's not his fault. He was raised that way. Come on, we'll walk you back to your trailer."

"You don't have to do that. I'm okay, honest." Arlene gave Charity an anxious glance. "You won't tell Newlin about what just happened, will you?"

Charity hesitated. "If that's what you want."

"What I really want is for Newlin to come with me on the spaceship." Arlene turned and trailed off into the shadows.

"I hope she's not going to be too depressed on Monday night when nothing happens," Charity said a short while later as she and Elias walked home.

"She'll have Newlin to comfort her."

Startled by the brusque tone of his voice, Charity gave him a searching look. It was impossible to see his expression in the darkness.

"Elias?"

"Yes?"

"You're sure you're okay? Rick didn't get a punch in, did he?"

"I'm okay."

Charity relaxed slightly. "That was very kind of you to go to Arlene's assistance."

Elias did not respond. He was obviously lost in his own churning thoughts.

Charity knew a no-trespassing sign when she saw one. She stopped talking and allowed the sounds of the night and the cove to fill the tense silence.

When they reached her cottage, she took out her key and walked up the porch steps to her front door. Elias made no attempt to follow her. He stood waiting at the bottom of the steps as she fitted her key into the lock.

She looked back at him as she opened the door, wondering what he would say if she invited him inside. The porch light etched his face in sharp, contrasting planes of light and shadow. He looked very remote, very distant. Back in control. She decided that in this mood he would refuse an offer of tea or a nightcap.

"Thanks for asking me to join you on your evening

walk." Deliberately she infused her voice with as much forced brightness as possible. "It was interesting, to say the least."

"Charity?"

She froze warily in the doorway. "Yes?"

"Did I scare you?"

Of all the things she might have expected him to say at that moment, his question was one she would never have imagined. "Scare me? You mean, with the way you tackled Rick Swinton? Don't be silly. Of course you didn't scare me. I was glad you tossed him out of the motor home. He deserved to land on his rear in the dirt. Arlene's right. He's a little twerp."

"I'm not talking about Swinton."

"Oh."

"I'm talking about us," Elias said very softly.

Her mouth went dry. She knew now that he was referring to the devastating intensity of the kiss they had shared. A kiss that had left him as shaken as it had her, she thought with rising satisfaction. Not that he would ever admit it.

Suddenly she felt incredibly cheerful. Incredibly sexy. Downright flirtatious. She folded her arms beneath her breasts and propped one shoulder against the doorjamb, trying for an air of unruffled, sophisticated aplomb.

"Do I look scared?" she asked.

"No."

She smiled. "What are you up to, Elias Winters?"

"Don't you know?"

"Enlighten me."

He held her eyes with unwavering intensity. There was no humor in that gaze. None at all. For Elias this was deadly serious, Charity realized. She felt a little sorry for him.

"I'm trying to start an affair with you," Elias said.

It took a determined effort, but she managed to get her mouth closed after a few stunned seconds. "I thought you were the subtle type."

"Is that an affirmative or a negative response?"

Charity struggled to maintain a few shreds of her composure. Damn if she would let him turn her into a babbling idiot. She took refuge in her old executive style.

"It's an I'll-get-back-to-you-on-that response," she said.

He nodded, accepting her words without comment. "Good night, Charity."

"Good night." Charity stepped back into the safety of her tiny hallway and very carefully closed and locked the door. Then she sagged weakly against it.

After a moment, she recovered sufficiently to go to the window and peek through the blinds. But she was too late to see Elias leave. He had already vanished into the night.

5

Volcanoes simmer beneath the deepest seas.
—"On the Way of Water," from the journal of Hayden Stone

He had not scared Charity, but he had certainly done a hell of a job scaring himself.

Two days later Elias still could not stop brooding over the kiss on the bluff.

He had just wanted to test the waters. Wade in the shallows. Check to see if the attraction was mutual. He had not expected to get caught by a riptide and swept out to sea before he knew what hit him.

Years of daily exercise, both physical and mental, designed to cultivate maximum internal balance and self-discipline, all gone in an instant. So much for playing it cool.

It had taken an hour of contemplation beside the garden pool, a cold shower, and a shot of whiskey to control the hungry need that had set his senses on edge Wednesday night. The temptation to walk back to Charity's cottage, knock on the door, and ask her to take him into her bed had nearly unhinged him.

Scary. Very scary.

But he was back in control now, he assured himself. Two days of intense Tal Kek Chara workouts had re-established the balance of his inner flow.

Sort of.

Elias stood behind his counter with Crazy Otis stationed beside him on the fake tree limb. Together they watched as Charity moved up and down the crowded aisles of Charms & Virtues, clipboard in hand.

With a woman like this, you had to be careful what you asked for, Elias reflected. This morning he had foolishly asked for some business marketing advice.

At the time he had been pleased with the subtle maneuver. He had thought to use the request as an excuse to spend more time with her. He had envisioned giving her tea in the intimate privacy of the tiny office behind the cash register counter.

But she had taken his request far too seriously. She was attacking the job of whipping his business into shape with gusto.

If she had experienced any serious aftereffects from that out-of-control kiss two days ago, they certainly didn't show, he thought morosely. "I'll get back to you on that," she had said when he'd told her that he wanted to have an affair. It was as if she had sensed the weakness in him and knew herself to be in the driver's seat.

Dangerous. But a challenge he could not resist.

"We'll have to find Hayden's supplier files and order info." Charity paused to pick up a pen off a stack marked *Spy Pens—Write Your Secret Messages in Invisible Ink.* "I have no idea where he got most of this stuff."

"There's a big stack of order catalogs in the office," Elias offered.

He studied the graceful, vulnerable curve of the nape of her neck. He was sorely tempted to come out from behind the barricade of the sales counter and see what would happen if he touched that sexy place beneath her hair. He resisted the urge. He had the raw fire of unrequited lust tamped down now, but the force of it was undiminished. Unfortunately the flames burned all the hotter for being banked.

Control was everything in Tal Kek Chara.

"Check the business records in his old filing cabinet. There should be invoices from the companies he used on a regular basis." Charity put aside the invisible ink pen and blew dust off a collection of tiny, carved wooden boxes. "I'll have Newlin bring over one of our extra feather dusters. A clean shop has eye appeal."

"I don't know." Elias surveyed the layer of grime on top of the fortune-teller's booth. "I think the dust adds atmosphere."

"That's ridiculous." Charity brushed her hands together. "It makes the place look untended. Also, you really should do something to improve the lighting in here. It looks like the inside of a cave."

"A couple of kids wandered in yesterday afternoon. I think they liked the spooky effect."

"Anything that makes it hard for your customers to see what you have to sell doesn't help business." Charity picked up a small box and probed curiously at the latch.

"Uh, Charity, be careful with that. Those little chests are filled with—"

"Don't get me wrong. I agree that it's a good idea to maintain an air of mystery in a shop like Charms &

Virtues, but you don't want to overdo it. Maybe some old-fashioned lamps, especially in the back section, would be the—aaaah!"

A large, furry spider leaped out of the box.

"Oh-my-god!" Charity shrieked again and hurled box and spider into the air.

"Heh-heh-heh." Crazy Otis sidled along his perch, shiny eyes glittering evilly.

"I tried to tell you." Elias came around from behind the counter and started down the aisle. "Those are gag boxes. They've all got fake spiders on springs stuffed inside."

Charity recovered quickly. "I should have known better than to fool around with any of this stuff." She shoved the spider back into the box and firmly closed the lid. "As long as I live, I will never understand the appeal of this type of merchandise."

"I think it's a kid thing."

"Well, as I was saying, I recommend that you get some attractive lighting fixtures in here as soon as possible. But first things first. You've got to dust." She broke off on a delicate sneeze.

"I'll see what I can do." He watched her yank a tissue out of her skirt pocket. "Charity, would you have dinner at my place with me tonight?"

Her eyes widened above the tissue that she held to her nose. "Dinner?"

The door swung open at that moment. Irritated by the interruption, Elias glanced toward the front of the shop. The last thing he wanted right now was a customer.

A florid-faced man dressed in gentlemen's-cut slacks, a white shirt that strained at the buttons, and taupe nubuck shoes stood in the entrance. His eyes gleamed determinedly behind the lenses of over-sized aviator glasses. He carried an expensive leather briefcase in one chubby hand. The square, diamond-studded ring on his left pinky was so large that Elias could see it very clearly from where he stood in the middle of the shop.

Charity blew her nose and turned quickly. "Oh, hello, Leighton. What are you doing here? Have you met Elias Winters? Elias, this is Leighton Pitt. The owner of Pitt Realty."

Elias nodded brusquely. "Pitt."

"Winters," Leighton sang out in a jovial voice that boomed off the walls. "Pleased to meet you." He started forward, broad hand outstretched.

Elias shook hands reluctantly and as briefly as possible. As he had feared, Leighton's palm was unpleasantly damp. As soon as the ancient ritual was completed, Elias surreptitiously wiped his hand off on the side of his jeans. He caught the amused glint in Charity's eyes just as he finished.

"Charity," Leighton turned to her. "Nice to see you. Fantastic day, isn't it? Been a chilly summer. Hope we get to keep this warm weather for a while."

"Good for business," Charity murmured politely.

"That it is, that it is." Leighton swung back to Elias. "Winters, you're just the man I want to see. Can you spare a few minutes? I'd like to talk to you about a business matter that I think you'll find very interesting."

"Can it wait?" Elias asked. "Charity was just giving me some tips on running this place."

Leighton winked broadly and chuckled. "As if you need consulting advice when it comes to business."

Charity glanced at her watch with an exaggerated expression of amazement. "Heavens, will you look at the time. Elias, I've got to run. I promised Newlin he could go to lunch early today. Arlene is coming over from the Voyagers' campground to join him."

"About tonight," Elias said grimly.

She gave him a brilliant smile. "As it happens, I'm free this evening."

"Six-thirty," he said swiftly. "I'll walk over and pick you up."

"That's not necessary. I can find my own way. Your place isn't that far from mine." She glanced at Leighton. "See you later, Leighton."

He gave her a brisk nod, his attention clearly focused on whatever presentation he planned to make to Elias. "You bet. Enjoy the great weather while you can."

Elias watched wistfully as Charity disappeared out the front door. She was wearing one of her floaty little cotton dresses again today, and the sunlight outside the shop revealed the sexy silhouette of her legs.

"Well, Winters, what say we get down to business, eh?"

Elias suppressed a groan as he turned back to his visitor. "If this is about real estate, I've already got a house."

"I know, Hayden Stone's old place out on the bluff." Leighton frowned. "You know, I could find you something in much better condition with a similar view."

"Don't bother. The cottage suits me just fine."

"Sure, you bet. That's not what I wanted to talk to you about today, anyway."

"What did you want to discuss?"

Leighton glanced toward the door as if to make certain that they were still alone. Then he winked again. His teeth sparkled in a confidential, man-to-man smile. "I know who you are, Winters, and I think I can guess why you're here in town."

"What a coincidence. I know who I am, too. And

I also know why I'm here. If that's all you wanted to talk about, I've got work to do."

"Hey, hey, hey." Leighton flapped his hand. "Take it easy. No offense intended. Just wanted you to realize that you're not the only one in town who knows the real score."

"Real score?"

"Look, I'll level with you." Leighton leaned in closer. The fragrance of a recently digested breath mint wafted through the air. "I'm aware that off-shore money is planning to move into Whispering Waters Cove in the next six months. I know all about the plans for a world-class resort and spa the company wants to develop here. Going to be built along the same lines as the properties the outfit developed in Hawaii, right? Except with an emphasis on golf instead of sunbathing, of course."

Elias held his breath to avoid inhaling the odor of mint. "Is that a fact?"

"No need to play dumb."

Elias thought of the kiss on the bluff. "But I do it so well."

"Sure, sure." Another wink. "I like a man with a sense of humor."

"No one's ever accused me of having one."

"Not everyone appreciates a keen wit." Sweat glistened on Leighton's brow. "Let's put our cards on the table. I know you own a consulting company called Far Seas, and I know just what kind of consulting you do. Only one reason you'd be here in our little town."

"What reason?"

Leighton gave him a very knowing look. "You're the advance man for the off-shore resort developer who wants to move in here to Whispering Waters Cove."

"I see."

"Don't worry." Leighton held up a plump hand. The huge diamond glittered. "I won't try to pin you down. No questions asked. Man in your position has to keep a low profile. But, frankly, I wondered when you or someone like you would show up."

"Did you?"

"Of course. Your client is getting ready to move. I just want you to know that you're not the only player in this situation. I've got a piece of the action, too. Or I will have, very soon."

"Uh-huh."

The smell of breath mint grew stronger as Leighton edged closer and lowered his voice. "Can't discuss the details yet. Like you, I've got to keep things quiet for a while longer. But I'll be able to speak more freely early next week. Bottom line here is that I'm the one you'll be dealing with when the ball starts rolling. Remember that."

"Be hard to forget."

Leighton chuckled. "You can say that again. Well, I'd better be going. Got an appointment. Just wanted to put you into the big picture before everything breaks loose. Hey, enjoy the weather. Summer doesn't usually last more than a few weeks around here."

"I'll keep that in mind."

"We'll talk later." Leighton turned and strode toward the door with a purposeful air. A man with a piece of the action. A player.

Crazy Otis shuffled back and forth on his perch and hissed softly.

Elias waited until Leighton had left the shop before he picked up the phone and dialed a familiar number in Seattle.

A woman answered in low, rich tones. "Thorgood,

Green, and Esteredge." She reeled off the names of the partners in the law firm as if they had each been canonized.

"Craig Thorgood, please."

"May I tell Mr. Thorgood who's calling?"

"Elias Winters."

"Just a moment, Mr. Winters."

Craig Thorgood came on the line. "What's up, Elias?"

His voice matched his office, rich and cultivated. The sort of voice that implied Thorgood had descended from several generations of old money and had followed a venerable family tradition when he had chosen to study law. Elias was one of the few people who knew that he had actually started out life on a farm in eastern Washington.

"Got time for a small job?"

"I've always got time to squeeze in a few extra billable hours. How small is the job?"

"I want you to find out whatever you can about a woman named Gwendolyn Pitt. Until a year ago she lived in Whispering Waters Cove. She's back here now, but I'd like to know where she's been for the past twelve months."

"What kind of business is she in?"

Elias heard a faint squeak on the other end of the line and knew that Craig was leaning back in his chair. "At the moment she's running a spaceship cult. But she used to be in real estate."

"Spaceship cult, huh? You do meet some interesting people in your line of work, Winters."

"You don't know the half of it. Give me a call when you get something."

"I will. How's the curio shop business?"

"Just the way I like it. Slow."

Craig laughed. "I give you six months at the outside. You'll be back in Seattle by the first of spring."

"I don't think so, Craig."

Charity showed up on the doorstep looking like the Spirit of Summer Night in a pale, high-waisted dress made of a fabric that seemed lighter than air. Elias felt his stomach knot with anticipation. The low, rounded neckline and little cap sleeves of her dress were at once flirtatious and innocent. Her auburn hair was done up in a casual twist that allowed little wispy tendrils to flutter around her cheeks.

She carried a bottle of chilled sauvignon blanc. Feminine mischief sparkled in her eyes. Elias knew that she was feeling very much in control of the situation. What really worried him was that he was half afraid she might be right. He drew a deep breath and summoned his resolve.

"I didn't know if white wine would work with whatever's on the menu tonight," she said as she handed him the bottle.

"This is a good night for sauvignon blanc." He took the wine and opened the door wide to usher her inside. "Come in."

"Thanks." She glanced down and smiled when she saw his bare feet. Without a word she stepped out of her sandals, placed them neatly beside the door, and walked into the small front room and glanced around curiously. "What did Leighton Pitt want this afternoon?"

"He admired my sense of humor among other things." Elias inhaled the scent of her as she brushed past him. The light skirt of her gauzy dress snagged briefly on his jeans. It was going to be a very long night.

"Free advice," Charity murmured. "Don't believe everything a salesman tells you."

"I'll remember that."

Crazy Otis, ensconced on top of his cage, looked up from the wooden toy he was busily gnawing. He eyed Charity with a hard stare and then muttered a churlish greeting.

"It's easy to see why some scientists think birds are related to dinosaurs," Charity remarked. "No manners at all."

Elias put the wine on the counter. "Otis said hello, didn't he?"

"Who knows what he said? All Crazy Otis does is mutter and cackle." Charity strolled over to the cage and surveyed Otis at close range. "But I have to admit that he's settled in quite nicely with you. I'm glad you two have hit it off. I was a tad worried about him for a while."

"If you hadn't taken him in, he probably would have gone under completely."

"I didn't really know what to do for a depressed parrot. I called a vet in Seattle, but he wasn't too helpful. So I just sort of followed my instincts."

Otis tilted his head to eye her more closely. "Heh-heh-heh."

Charity made a face. "Not that you've ever shown so much as an ounce of gratitude, Otis."

"He's just too proud to admit he needed you," Elias said.

"Yeah, right. You know, Hayden once told me that Otis could talk, but I've never heard him do anything except chuckle and hiss and mutter unintelligibly."

Elias opened a drawer to find a corkscrew. "I'm sure Otis will talk if he ever has anything to say."

"I won't hold my breath." Charity turned away from Otis to examine the spare room. "I see your furniture hasn't arrived yet. You should have said something. I could loan you a couple of chairs and a table. I brought all my stuff from Seattle."

"I appreciate the offer, but I don't need any more furniture."

That wasn't strictly true, he thought as he went to work with the corkscrew. A slightly larger bed would have been nice. Making love to Charity on the narrow futon would be a challenge. Of course, he wasn't going to have to worry about it tonight. Control was everything in Tal Kek Chara.

"I suppose this, uh, minimalist style goes with the obscure water philosophy."

"Tal Kek Chara. Yes."

"Tal Kek Chara. Is that what you call it?"

"Loosely translated, it means the Way of Water. The literal translation is a lot more complicated." Elias suddenly realized that now that Hayden was dead, he was probably the only person left in the states who knew the exact translation of the ancient words. It was an eerie, lonely feeling.

"I see." Charity leaned down to touch the heavy glass bowl half-filled with water that sat on the low table. "This is a nice piece. Very nice."

Elias looked across the room to where she stood gazing down into the bowl. Something twisted inside him. "I gave it to Hayden a few years ago."

"He obviously treasured it." She ran her fingertip meditatively along the rim of the thick glass. "It's the only decorative item in the room."

Elias thought about that. "I guess he must have liked it." The tightness inside him relaxed. She was right. Hayden must have valued the bowl very highly to have kept it here in this otherwise spartan room.

Charity wandered across the small space to the kitchen area. "We were discussing Leighton. Did he compliment you on your humor in order to try to sell you some real estate today?"

"No. He informed me that he's a player."

"A player?"

"A mover-and-shaker. Wheeler-dealer. Big man here in town. A guy in the know."

"Hmm. Any particular reason why he would make a special trip down to the pier to announce that to you?"

Elias took two glasses out of the cupboard. "He seems to think that things are going to get hot here in Whispering Waters Cove."

She shrugged. "That's certainly what the town council hopes will happen."

"Pitt implied that he knows something specific. He says an off-shore developer intends to put in a golf resort and spa."

"A resort? That's specific, all right." Charity watched him fill the glasses with the cool sauvignon blanc. Her eyes were thoughtful and just a little wary. "Do you think Leighton knows what he's talking about?"

"Can't say." He handed her a glass. "But I'll lay odds that whatever he thinks is going on is tied to his ex-wife's spaceship cult."

She met his eyes. "Not to you?"

"Not to me."

"Interesting. That brings up the question of what's going to happen on Monday."

"I called a friend of mine in Seattle, a lawyer named Thorgood. Specializes in corporate law. His firm employs a whole fleet of researchers and investigators. I asked him to see if he can find out what Gwendolyn Pitt has been up to during the past few months."

"Things are getting more and more mysterious, aren't they?"

"They may be a lot simpler than they seem." Elias leaned back against the counter and took a sip of the wine. It was spicy and tantalizing on his tongue. Just like Charity. "Sounds like it may come down to money, after all."

"Guess we'll just have to wait until Monday night to see what happens." Charity's eyes gleamed over the rim of her wine glass. "Whoever said small town life wasn't exciting?"

"Not me." He looked at her and suddenly could not look away.

The air became more dense between them. The invisible currents moving through it were charged with a spectrum of possibilities. There was no rush, he reminded himself. No rush at all. He would not allow himself to be swept away by the tide.

Charity blinked first. "What's for dinner?"

"Artichoke dip with toasted pita bread. Gorgonzola and spinach ravioli, hearts of romaine salad, and some hazelnut gelati with biscotti for dessert."

Her eyes widened. "I'm impressed."

He savored her astonished wonder. "I'll admit that I was surprised to find the biscotti in the Whispering Waters Cove Grocery."

"You reaped the results of my months of negotiations with the grocery store manager. Mr. Gedding and I have a deal. He stocks the items I request, and I pay rip-off prices for them."

"Fair enough."

Laughter lit her eyes. She batted her lashes. "Have I ever told you how much I admire a man who can cook?"

"I don't believe you've mentioned it." He put his glass down on the counter and turned to the stove. "But feel free to hold forth on the subject."

"Okay. I deeply, deeply admire a man who can cook."

She was flirting again. A good sign, Elias thought. This was right where he wanted to be. The trick was to stay here in the shallows where they could both have some fun without any danger of getting in too deep.

"I'll try not to take advantage of your vulnerability to good cooks," he said as he set a large pan of water on the old stove. "How's Newlin doing?"

The mischief faded from her eyes. "I'm a little worried about him. He's afraid of what Arlene will do when the spaceships fail to show. I wish I could reassure him that everything will be all right, but the truth is, I don't know how she'll handle reality when it strikes."

"We'll keep an eye on Newlin," Elias promised. He realized as he spoke the words that he was starting to identify himself as a member of the Crazy Otis Landing gang. It was a strange sensation, but not unpleasant.

He took Charity home shortly after eleven. It was all very proper, very old-fashioned.

It was not, however, very easy.

The waves of sensual tension had grown stronger as the evening progressed. All throughout dinner she had watched him with an intriguing combination of shy anticipation and womanly knowledge in her eyes. Elias knew that she had been waiting for him to make the first move, the one that would lead to the bedroom.

It took a valiant effort to suggest that it was getting late and that it was time to return her to her own cottage. The surprise that flashed briefly across her face was almost enough to comfort the regret he knew he would feel later. Almost, but not quite.

Elias covered Otis's cage and stepped into his shoes. He paused to pick up the flashlight, but they did not need it. A partial moon and a sky full of stars provided enough illumination to see the bluff path. Across the cove the lights of the town and Crazy Otis Landing sparkled in the distance.

Charity's arm, tucked inside Elias's, was warm and supple and softly rounded. He could smell the scent of her shampoo. Something herbal, he concluded. It mingled with the balmy sea breeze and her own unique fragrance. The sum of the ingredients created a potent dish that aroused his hunger.

A balanced flow had to be restored in this relationship, he reminded himself. He had to stay centered. Hayden's words echoed in his head. *He who knows the Way of Water lets his opponent come to him.* A man and a woman hovering on the brink of an affair were adversaries whether or not they acknowledged it. Each wanted something from the other. Each had an agenda.

The good-night kiss at the door was tricky, but Elias had braced himself for it. He brushed her mouth lightly with his own. When she started to put her hands on his shoulders, he took a half step back. Her arms fell to her side.

"I'll see you in the morning," he said.

She watched him through the veil of her half-lowered lashes. "Thanks for dinner. It was wonderful. Can I return the favor on Monday night?"

Satisfaction blossomed inside him. "I'll look forward to it."

"Afterward we can walk down to the Voyagers' campground and watch the starships arrive." She grinned. "I'm sure everyone in town will be there. Fun for the whole family. Better than the county fair."

"Never a dull moment in Whispering Waters Cove."

"Tell me, Elias, if the ships do happen to show up as advertised, will you be tempted to leave with the aliens?"

"No." He looked into her eyes and felt the heat rise. "Something tells me that the answers I want are here, not somewhere out in space."

She stilled. "Are you sure of that?"

"Very sure. But I haven't finished asking all the questions yet. Good night, Charity." It was time to go. He had to get off her porch before the riptide caught him again and carried him back out to sea. He turned and went resolutely down the steps.

"Elias?"

Her soft, husky voice brought him to a halt. He looked back at her. "What is it?"

"Did you prove your point?"

"What point?"

"The one you've been trying to prove all evening." She gave him a rueful smile. "That you're back in control? That even though things got a little exciting out there on the bluff the other night, you're still Joe Cool?"

"Ah, that point." He should have known that she'd guessed what was going on. "Maybe."

"Having fun yet?"

"No, but it builds character."

She laughed and shut the door in his face.

Elias realized he was grinning like an idiot. A joke. That was definitely a joke. Maybe not a great joke, but still, what could you expect from a man who was new at this kind of thing.

He backed away from the porch, turned, and broke into an easy, loping run. With any luck, he could work off some of the excess sexual energy that was charging his senses with lightning.

In spite of the ache that desire had created in his

lower body, he felt good. Better than he had since Hayden had died. Better than he had in years. He ran faster. Below the bluff, silver moonlight played on the waters of the cove. The air was a tonic in his blood. The night stretched out forever.

He ran for a long time before he slowed to a walk, turned, and started back toward his darkened cottage.

He saw the movement at the window just as he reached the garden gate. He came to a halt and stood quietly in the dense shadow of a madrona tree. He watched with interest as a dark figure scrambled out over the sill.

The intruder grunted when he landed, panting, on the porch. As soon as he caught his balance, he started to struggle frantically with the raised window.

"Shit." The expletive was a low, muttered exclamation.

Elias recognized the voice. Rick Swinton.

Swinton finally closed the window with one last, anxious shove. He swung around and dashed down the porch steps into the garden. There was a splash as he blundered straight into the reflecting pool.

"Goddamn it." Swinton hauled himself out of the shallow pool and tore down the path, wet chinos flapping. He never saw Elias standing quietly in the thick darkness created by the madrona tree.

Elias could have reached out and touched him. Or stuck out a foot and sent Swinton sprawling. He did neither.

Instead, he followed his uninvited guest at a discreet distance. Swinton ran around to the front of the cottage and pounded down the narrow, tree-lined drive that led back to the main road.

His car was parked behind a stand of fir trees. He yanked open the door, leaped into the driver's seat, and started the engine. He did not turn on his head-lights until he was a hundred yards down the road.

Elias waited at the edge of the drive for a few min-utes, curious to see whether Swinton would head back toward the Voyagers' compound or into town. The headlights turned left when they reached the intersec-tion. Toward Whispering Waters Cove.

Elias walked slowly back to the cottage. He went up the porch steps and opened the front door. He removed his shoes and went into the house.

Crazy Otis was muttering anxiously beneath his cov-ered cage.

"It's all right, Otis. I'm here."

Otis calmed and then, true to form, turned a bit surly. "Hsss."

"My sentiments, exactly." Elias did not turn on the lights. He went to the window Swinton had used for his breaking and entering. "He either got lucky or he was watching the place all evening. When he saw me leave to take Charity home, he probably assumed I'd spend the night at her place."

"Heh-heh-heh."

"Yeah. Heh-heh-heh. Little did he know that I was using the evening as a Tal Kek Chara exercise in self-discipline and restraint." Elias gazed out into the night. "Idiot." He paused. "In case you're wondering, Otis, I was referring to myself, not Swinton."

"Heh-heh-heh."

Elias walked through the small cottage. The bare decor left few potential hiding places. It would not have taken Swinton long to go through the limited possibilities.

"I don't like guests who forget to remove their shoes, Otis."

Elias was not surprised to see that the only thing that appeared to have been disturbed was the carved chest in the bedroom. One glance inside revealed that Swinton had pawed through the contents.

The one item in the chest that Elias cared about, Hayden Stone's journal, was still safe at the bottom. He picked it up and turned it in his hands. He had not been able to bring himself to read it yet.

He replaced the journal and closed the lid of the chest slowly. It was possible that, having struck out at the house, Swinton had headed into town in order to break into Charms & Virtues. Elias hoped he wouldn't make too much of a mess.

"Everyone here in Whispering Waters Cove seems to think I'm a man of mystery, Otis." He went into the bathroom to turn on the shower. "Hope they're not too disappointed when they find out I'm just an innocent, hardworking shopkeeper with no ulterior real estate motives."

"Heh-heh-heh."

Elias emerged from the shower a few minutes later. He rolled out the futon and settled down on it. He folded his arms behind his head and contemplated the shadowy ceiling.

"So, Otis, what was it like, sleeping in Charity's bedroom?"

"Heh-heh-heh."

6

———⁊⁊⁊———

Water is deepest beneath the place where it appears the
most calm on the surface.

—"On the Way of Water," from the journal of Hayden Stone

The sight of Phyllis Dartmoor striding briskly into
Whispers on Saturday morning did not brighten Charity's day. The mayor of Whispering Waters Cove
looked even more determined and aggressive than
usual. Charity wished she could duck out of the back
door, but there wasn't time.

That would have been the coward's way out, anyway, she told herself. It was just unfortunate that she'd
had very little sleep, having spent the long night instead lying awake, trying to analyze Elias.

It had not been a productive task. She had replayed
the final scene at her front door a thousand times, and
by dawn she had been forced to conclude that she'd
had a narrow escape.

Sure, she had laughed at the time, even teased Elias. But in the cold, harsh light of day, it was clear that she had been in an unfamiliar, extraordinarily reckless mood last night. Make that the whole of the last week. Playing with fire, that's what she was doing. Not like her at all. That kiss on the bluff a few days ago had done weird things to her.

Amazing what could happen to one's normal sense of caution when one realized that one no longer suffered from panic attacks in a man's embrace.

Today it was breathtakingly obvious that she could easily have been swept up into a very dangerous liaison last night. And it would have been her own fault. She had spent the whole evening flirting outrageously. She had wanted Elias to lose control again, the way he had on the bluff. She had wanted to see the passion flare in his eyes, feel his strong, sexy hands on her, know that she could turn him on.

Thank heavens Elias had been into his Zenny-mode last night. In his effort to affirm his own prodigious powers of self-control, he had given her a chance to come to her senses.

Breathing space. That was what he had inadvertently given her last night. Breathing space. This morning she was resolved to take advantage of it.

She needed time. She needed to think things through. Before she made any major moves, she needed to know a hell of a lot more about Elias Winters. She must remember Davis's advice. *Watch your step with Winters. Rumor has it he's not just a player, he's a winner. Every time.*

No two ways about it, she'd had a very close call.

Whatever was fated to happen between herself and Elias would definitely have to be postponed until they were better acquainted. Much better acquainted.

Blah, blah, blah.

She'd been giving herself the same lecture for hours. The words were a litany in her brain. She was beginning to sound like Crazy Otis.

"Good morning, Charity." The heels of Phyllis's Italian pumps clicked sharply on the shop floor.

"Hello, Phyllis." Charity stationed herself squarely behind the counter. "Something tells me you didn't come in to buy a book. Are you here on business or politics?"

"A little of both." Phyllis came to a halt and favored Charity with a cool smile that was all width and no depth. It was a practiced, charming smile that showed a lot of white, capped teeth.

It would have been easy to dislike Phyllis, Charity thought. After all, the two of them had become fierce adversaries as they did battle over the fate of Crazy Otis Landing. Their confrontations at town council meetings had already become legendary in Whispering Waters Cove. But Charity had been cursed from Day One of their association with a deeply rooted sense of sympathy for her new nemesis.

She knew her empathy was ridiculous, and she took great pains to conceal it, but she was unable to shake it. Phyllis reminded her of the person she, herself, had once been. A classic overachiever. A driven workaholic, obsessively goal-oriented. She wondered if Phyllis had ever had a panic attack.

Phyllis had a law degree from the University of Washington. She ran her own law practice in Whispering Waters Cove. She fulfilled her duties as town mayor with tireless energy. In her free time she campaigned for all the right candidates in state elections and got herself invited to the right cocktail parties in Seattle and Olympia.

She was a tall, sleek woman in her mid-thirties. Her sophistication would have caused her to stand out in

Seattle. In a small town like Whispering Waters Cove, she stood out so much she looked out of place.

Phyllis was the only woman in town who habitually wore a suit. Today's version had been crisply tailored in summer-weight linen that was already properly crumpled even though it was only five minutes after ten. The jacket was equipped with impressive shoulder pads that gave her figure a strong forties' silhouette.

Phyllis drove to Seattle every month to have her light brown hair cut in a dashing wedge. After Jennifer Pitt had given every woman in town a taste for sculpted nails, Phyllis had become a regular at Nails by Radiance. The special color Radiance had created for her was called Dartmoor Mauve.

"Are you alone?" Phyllis glanced around the obviously empty bookshop.

"At the moment. My assistant went to get himself an iced latte at Bea's place and it's a little early for weekend tourists. What can I do for you?"

"I wanted to talk to you about the new owner of Crazy Otis Landing."

"Why don't you talk to him, instead?"

"I've already tried that." Phyllis's mouth tightened. "He was civil but completely uncooperative. Kept wanting to discuss water, of all things."

"You went to see Elias?" Charity was horrified by the very unpleasant twinge that shot through her. She prayed it was not jealousy.

"Ran into him at the post office. He acted totally disinterested in what I had to say."

Charity relaxed a little. "So? What do you expect me to do?"

Phyllis lowered her voice to a gratingly confidential tone. "I understand the two of you are seeing each other."

"Every day." Charity smiled blandly. "Can't miss

each other, what with both of us running shops right here on the same pier."

"That's not what I meant, and I think you know it." A steely expression appeared in Phyllis's eyes. "The rumor is that you've started seeing him socially."

Charity was amazed. She had made no effort to keep last night's date a secret, but she certainly hadn't broadcast the news, either. Elias must have mentioned their dinner to someone, who had, in turn, spread it immediately all over the cove.

"Nothing like a small town for gossip, is there?" Charity muttered.

"Look, I'll be blunt. It's common knowledge that Winters is not just the new proprietor of that ridiculous curio shop at the other end of the pier. He's the new owner of this entire landing." Phyllis leaned closer. "And, he's also the head of a very high-stakes consulting company called Far Seas, Inc."

"So?"

"So he's a player. The question is, what game is he playing?"

Charity smiled grimly. "Whatever it is, I can guarantee that he's writing his own rules."

"That doesn't surprise me." Phyllis tapped one long, Dartmoor Mauve nail on the counter. "Winters is up to something. There's a lot of speculation going on, but the bottom line is that no one really knows what he intends to do with the Landing. That's why we need your help."

"We?"

"Those of us who care about the future of this town. You're the only one who's established any sort of relationship with him."

"Phyllis, I don't know what the rumors were like by the time they reached you, but I can assure you that it was just dinner, not an engagement party."

"Look, this isn't a joke. No one else around here can get a straight answer out of Winters."

"He doesn't exactly specialize in straight answers," Charity admitted.

"You know as well as I do that the town council has had its eye on Crazy Otis Landing for some time now. Hayden Stone was impossible. As long as he owned the pier, there was no hope of upgrading the shops. But now that he's gone, we want to convince Winters that it's in his own best interests to cooperate with the council's plans."

"There's that word 'we' again. It makes me nervous."

"The members of the council and I want you to join our team, Charity. It's time we stopped arguing about the future of this pier and worked together to make it the centerpiece of the new Whispering Waters Cove."

"I like it the way it is."

"Where's your sense of vision?" Phyllis demanded. "You were once a successful businesswoman. With the obvious exception of Elias Winters, you're the only one on this pier with a head for business. The rest of these misfits couldn't make a profit running a hotdog stand at a Fourth of July Parade."

Charity felt her temper stir. Sooner or later it always came down to this with Phyllis. "The shopkeepers of Crazy Otis Landing are not misfits. They've single-handedly kept this pier alive for the town for the past twenty years. Everyone else considered it an eyesore until recently."

"Alive?" Phyllis waved one beautifully manicured hand in an exasperated gesture. "You call this alive? You've got three shops standing empty. They've been empty for years."

"We'll get them rented sooner or later."

"No smart businessperson is going to open a store

on this pier until there's some guarantee that the image of the landing will be improved."

"You don't have to evict all of the present tenants in order to improve the landing," Charity snapped. "We're doing a good job of building business all by ourselves. Foot traffic here on the pier has tripled this summer. Bea's pulling in tourists with her espresso machine. Radiance has brought in local people with her nail parlor. Yappy's booked several birthday parties down at the carousel. Ted's T-shirt sales have skyrocketed. And I'm doing just fine with my bookstore, thank you very much."

"You can't stand in the way of progress, for God's sake."

"I can stand anywhere I like."

Phyllis drew an audible breath. "I didn't come here to argue with you."

"Really? I would never have guessed."

"Be reasonable, Charity. I came to enlist you on the side of the future. We need your help. You stand to benefit from a revitalized pier as much as anyone does. This bookshop of yours would work beautifully in an upscale version of Crazy Otis Landing. Help us convince Winters to cooperate."

Charity leaned both elbows on the counter and clasped her hands. She eyed Phyllis with a mixture of caution and growing fascination. "Let us say, for the sake of argument, that I was willing to help you accomplish your plans. How, exactly, do you expect me to convince Elias to cooperate with the council?"

Phyllis pounced on the small opening. "We need you to talk to him. Find out what he plans to do with the pier. We want to work with him."

"Work with him?"

"We're all interested in upgrading Crazy Otis Landing. If he's brokering a deal for off-shore investors,

which is what Leighton Pitt implies, we need to
know that."

Charity stared at her in growing amazement. "You
want me to spy for you."

Phyllis scowled, then turned red beneath her
makeup. "You're overdramatizing this, Charity. We're
just asking you to do your civic duty."

"Hmm. Did you ever see an old Hitchcock film
called *Notorious?* Forties' spy thriller with Cary Grant
and Ingrid Bergman? Ingrid has to seduce and marry
the bad guy in order to keep tabs on him. Everyone
tells her it's her duty."

Phyllis's eyes narrowed. "I fail to see the rele-
vance."

"I guess you're right. I really don't look much like
Ingrid Bergman, do I?" She broke off when she realized that Newlin was standing in the doorway behind Phyllis.

Newlin hesitated, latte cup in hand. "Want me to
wait outside, Charity?"

"It's okay, Newlin." Charity smiled at him. "The
mayor and I have finished our little chat."

Phyllis frowned at Newlin. Then she turned back to
Charity. "Think about what I said. This is important
to all of us. The future of this town may very well
depend on what you decide to do."

"Just this town? Gee, I dunno, Phyllis. Anything
less than the fate of the free world seems like a waste
of my talents."

"You're being extremely shortsighted." Phyllis
whirled and strode out of the shop without another
word.

Newlin wandered back behind the counter. "Some-
thin' wrong?"

"Nothing more than usual. The mayor is concerned
about the pier."

"She ought to spend more time worryin' about having Hank Tybern arrest Gwendolyn Pitt."

"Gwendolyn Pitt isn't doing anything illegal," Charity pointed out gently.

"Well, it oughta be illegal." Newlin gulped down half of the iced latte. "The mayor sure worked hard enough to get rid of those Voyagers when they first moved into town. Remember how at the beginning of July she was always sendin' Tybern out to hassle 'em about health and safety violations?"

"I remember."

"Then she just backed off for some reason."

"Very wise of her. Phyllis came to the obvious conclusion that there wasn't much she could do except wait it out. With any luck, the Voyagers will disband after the spaceships fail to show."

"Maybe." Newlin's jaw tensed. "Maybe not. Folks can be real weird about stuff like that. Gwendolyn Pitt has a lot to answer for, if you ask me. Someone oughta do something about her. It ain't right. It just ain't right."

Shortly before four o'clock, Elias hung up the new feather duster Charity had given him and looked at Crazy Otis.

"I've had it with the housecleaning. I still say Charity's wrong. A little dust makes the place more interesting."

Otis mumbled a response.

"There isn't a customer in sight. I think we've had our rush for the day." Elias moved closer to the perch. "Want to go see how Yappy's doing on those repairs to the carousel?"

Otis bobbed his head and stepped onto Elias's shoulder with regal dignity.

Elias strolled out of the shop, turned right, and

headed toward the far end of the pier. He was feeling good today. The ebullient sense of anticipation that had descended on him last night still held in spite of the fact that he had been right about Rick Swinton.

Swinton had, indeed, paid a visit to the small back office of Charms & Virtues after making his late-night visit to the cottage. But other than scattering the contents of the trash can, which Swinton had apparently tripped over at some point, no damage had been done. Elias wondered what his midnight visitor had made of the mundane collection of invoices, catalogs, order forms, and sales receipts that filled the small file cabinet.

Elias made a note to call Craig Thorgood and have him look into Swinton's background, as well as Gwendolyn Pitt's.

The pier had been busy earlier in the day, but things had tapered off after four. Elias saw Newlin working at the counter of Whispers when he went past the shop. Newlin looked grim, as usual. There was no sign of Charity.

Elias strolled past the three unrented shops and paused. It would be a good idea to get tenants into the empty spaces, he thought. He'd have to see about the matter.

"How's it hangin', Winters?" Ted waved from the doorway of Ted's Instant Philosophy T-Shirts. He had a new paperback mystery novel in one hand. A bookmark bearing the Whispers logo stuck out from between the pages.

As usual, Ted wore one of his own products. The T-shirt, which did not quite cover his belly, bore the advice, *Be Good. If You Can't Be Good, Be Careful.*

"Business is a little slow right now," Elias said. "Otis and I thought we'd take a walk."

"Things'll pick up tomorrow."

"Right."

Bea nodded to Elias as she poured iced tea for a customer seated at an outside table. Radiance gave him the old sixties' peace sign through the beaded curtain of Nails by Radiance.

It occurred to Elias that even though he had been here less than two weeks, he was developing the strange feeling that he actually belonged here on the pier. For once he was not standing entirely apart from everyone else, watching them from the balanced place inside himself. He was sharing some of the same space the others shared.

It was as if the river of his life had flowed around an unexpected bend and mingled with some of the same streams that flowed through the lives of some of the others.

He was not certain how to evaluate the change that was taking place. In a way it seemed to go against his training. On the other hand, it felt right. He wished Hayden were still alive so that he could ask him about the strange sensation. There were so many questions he would have liked to ask Hayden.

Elias reached the end of the pier and discovered Yappy deep in the guts of the carousel machinery. The colorful horses were frozen in a circle around him.

"Hey there, Winters." Yappy waved a wrench in greeting.

"How's it going?" Elias stepped up onto the platform and propped one shoulder against the hindquarters of a flying horse. Otis stepped off onto the horse's tail, settled his feathers, and prepared to supervise the work in progress.

"Gettin' there," Yappy said.

Elias studied the inside drive mechanism with interest. "Find the trouble?"

"Yeah, I think so. Should have it running again in a few more minutes. Hand me a screwdriver, will you?"

Elias glanced at the array of tools lying on a small bench. "Which one?"

"Phillips head."

Elias picked up the screwdriver and slapped it into Yappy's grease-stained palm. "Going down to the beach to see the Voyagers off Monday night?"

"Wouldn't miss it." Yappy twirled the screwdriver with expert precision. "Whole town's going to be there. Or at least, a good percentage. Bea plans to set up a refreshment stand. Sell some coffee, soda. Maybe some muffins. Figure I'll give her a hand. What about you?"

"I'll be there."

Yappy paused long enough to shoot Elias a speculative look. "With Charity?"

"Yes."

"You two are getting kind of close, aren't you?"

"Is that a problem?"

"No, I guess not." Yappy sounded thoughtful. "Your business."

"That's the way I look at it."

"Just so you know," Yappy continued in a slow, deliberate drawl. "We're all real fond of Charity around here. None of us would take kindly to seeing her hurt, if you take my meaning."

"I think I know what you're trying to say. But she's not a kid. She can take care of herself."

"She's got a head on her shoulders, all right," Yappy conceded. "Knows what she's doing when it comes to running a business. She's the one who came up with the notion of renting out the carousel for catered birthday parties. Doubled my profits this summer. She gave Radiance the idea of creating a special nail color for every one of her regular customers, too. Worked like a charm."

"It's obvious that Charity has good marketing instincts."

"Damn right. Understands how to deal with the local politicos, too. Kept the town council off our backs until you showed up. But when it comes to other stuff, she's not quite so tough."

"What do you mean?"

"Bea told me that Charity went through a real nasty episode just before she came here. Broke up with some rich guy in Seattle named Loftus."

"Brett Loftus."

"Know him?"

"Saw him once." Elias recalled the business luncheon where the blond, blue-eyed, square-jawed Loftus had entertained a crowd of bankers and investors with witty stories and incisive insights into the murky world of the athletic sportswear business. Elias had thought about that luncheon a lot lately. Ever since Charity had mentioned Loftus, in fact.

"Yeah, well, she hasn't dated anyone since she hit Whispering Waters Cove. Least not that Bea and I know about."

"Until I came along."

"Uh-huh." Yappy peered at him through a maze of gears. "Until you came along."

"I appreciate your concern for her, Yappy. Tell me, is anyone equally concerned about me?"

"Figure you can take care of yourself." Yappy wiped his grimy hands on the leg of his pants. "That should do it." He stepped out of the drive house, closed the panel, and pulled a lever. "We'll give Otis a test ride."

Otis cackled with glee as the bright, gem-studded horses began to glide in a circle. He gripped the saddle of a gleaming Pegasus with his powerful claws and shook out his brilliant feathers.

"Old Otis really gets a kick out of this." Yappy shook his head. "Charity used to bring him down here after Hayden died. We all thought that bird was a goner. Real sad sight. No spirit at all. But Charity pulled him out of it."

"She thinks that Otis isn't properly appreciative, but I'm sure he's grateful."

Yappy snorted. "Yeah. Right."

Elias watched the boy from the shadows behind the counter. The kid looked to be about nine years old. He wore the universal boy uniform: a pair of jeans, sneakers, and a T-shirt.

It had been a long, lazy Sunday. Elias glanced at the cuckoo clock. It was five-twenty-five. Almost closing time. The kid had been in the shop for nearly half an hour, and thus far he had made a trip up and down every single aisle, methodically examining the entire inventory.

"Was there something special you wanted?" Elias finally asked.

The boy jumped in surprise. He turned quickly to gaze into the dark area at the rear of the shop. Elias realized the kid hadn't noticed him until that moment.

The boy shook his head quickly and took a step back. "Uh, no. I was just kinda lookin' around."

"Okay." Elias held out his arm to Crazy Otis, who stepped aboard.

The boy flinched at the movement and took another step back toward the front door.

Way to go Winters, Elias thought. Scare off the customers.

He picked up the glass of water he had poured earlier for himself and walked slowly around the edge of the counter. The boy watched uneasily. He looked as if he was about to turn and flee. Then he saw Otis. His eyes widened.

"Is he real?"

"Yes." Elias reached up to scratch Otis's head. The parrot stretched languidly.

"Wow." The boy stopped edging backward. "Does he talk?"

"When he feels like it." Elias moved closer. "Did you see the invisible-ink pens over there?"

The kid looked both fascinated and uncertain. "No."

"They really work." Elias came to a halt beside the stack of pens. "Watch." He selected one and jotted a few words on a pad of demonstration paper. "See? Nothing shows."

The kid frowned dubiously. "How do you make the writing visible?"

"You dip the paper into a glass of water that has a few drops of this stuff in it." Elias held up a small vial that contained the harmless chemical mixture.

He unscrewed the top of the tiny bottle and sprinkled a couple of drops of the contents into the glass he held. Then he put the small page of paper into the water.

The boy shifted and drew closer. "Let me see."

Elias pulled the paper out of the water with a flourish and held it out. The words *Buy this pen* were clearly visible.

"Cool." The boy looked up eagerly. "Can I try it?"

"Sure." Elias handed over the pen and the small vial.

"This is great, man." The youngster scribbled busily on the pad of paper. "I can't wait to show it to Alex."

"Alex?"

"Yeah, he's my best friend. Me and him are going

down to the beach Monday night to see if the spaceships come. My Dad's going to take us."

"I'll be there, too."

"Yeah?" The boy squinted thoughtfully. "Think the
aliens will show?"

"No."

The kid sighed. "That's what my Dad says. But it
would sure be neat if they did land, wouldn't it?"

"It would be interesting."

"It'd be so cool." The kid's enthusiasm lit his eyes.
"If they did come, I'd go into outer space with 'em."

"Why?"

"Huh?" The boy scowled at the question. "On account of they'd have such great stuff. Just think about
what their computers would be like. Way ahead of
ours. They'd know the answers to everything."

"No, they wouldn't."

The kid looked taken aback. "Why not?"

"Because technology, no matter how advanced, can
never supply all the answers. Some things you have to
learn on your own. Even the most powerful computers
wouldn't change that."

"You sure?"

"Yes." Elias looked at the pen. "That'll be two-
ninety-eight plus tax. No charge for the philosophical
sound bite."

"What's a philosophical sound bite?"

"A personal opinion." Elias led the way back to the
cash register. "That's why I'm not charging you for it."

"Oh." The boy dug into his pocket for the money.
"Are you open Sundays?"

"During the summer."

"Great. I'm going to bring Alex here tomorrow."

"If you do, I'll give you a free replacement bottle
of invisible ink."

"Cool." The boy grabbed the paper sack that contained his new pen and the little vial and raced toward the door.

He had to dash around Charity, who had obviously been watching the transaction. She waited until Elias's young customer had vanished, and then she walked toward the counter. Her eyes sparkled with amusement.

"You look pleased with yourself," she said.

Elias gazed thoughtfully at the empty doorway. "I think that kid is going to enjoy that pen."

"I believe you're right. I told you, it's a calling."

"What is?"

"Running a shop like this. Not everyone is cut out for it. My sister or someone like Phyllis Dartmoor, for example, wouldn't be happy operating something this small. Give either of them Charms & Virtues and neither would rest until she had turned it into a coast-to-coast chain. I would have done the same thing, myself, until last summer."

Elias smiled. "Maybe I would have, too."

"Some people," Charity said deliberately, "have to keep pushing and expanding until they've got a universe to control. They don't know how to be content with just one small, complete world."

Elias picked up a sack of bird feed and began to refill Otis's cup. "Is that a not very subtle way of asking me if I'm going to be able to settle down here in a small place like Whispering Waters Cove and find satisfaction with a shop such as Charms & Virtues?"

Charity frowned. "I thought I was being extremely subtle."

"If that's your idea of subtlety, you've forgotten everything you must have once known about the subject."

"Dang. Are you sure it wasn't subtle?"

"Afraid not." Elias refolded the bag and stashed it under the perch.

"Well, shoot. I guess this means I'm not going to be able to do my civic duty and sacrifice myself for the good of Whispering Waters Cove, after all."

Elias paused. "What sort of duty and sacrifice did you have in mind?"

"It was recently suggested to me by Her Honor, the Mayor, that I use my amazing powers of seduction to persuade you to tell me the nature of your secret plans. I have been instructed to use my womanly wiles to find out exactly what you're up to here in Whispering Waters Cove."

"In the words of my last customer: cool."

"Naturally, my first thought was of Ingrid Bergman in *Notorious.*"

"Sounds like we're on the same wavelength here."

She frowned. "Things were going great until you said I lacked subtlety. What good is an unsubtle spy?"

"Maybe you just need a little experience," Elias said. "I might be willing to let you practice on me."

"Really?"

The phone rang in the small office. Elias held up a hand. "Hold that thought. I'll be right back."

"Yeah, sure. That's what they all say. Sorry, I can't hang around. Got to go close up for the day." Charity started to turn away. "Six-thirty Monday night okay for dinner?"

"I'll bring the wine this time."

"See you." She waved as she hurried out through the front door.

Elias grinned as he scooped up the phone. He had never had much inclination to play the flirtation game in the past, but he thought he might be able to get into the spirit of the thing with Charity.

"Charms & Virtues. Winters here."

"Elias? This is Craig. Got a minute?"

"Sure." Elias leaned out of the doorway of his office and watched Charity stride past the shop window. Her long yellow cotton dress flitted with the breeze, revealing the sweet hollows at the back of her knees. "Get anything on Gwen Pitt?"

"As a matter of fact, I did. She's been a busy woman during the past year."

"Doing what?"

"What she does best, apparently. Buying and selling Northwest real estate. The interesting part is that she's been doing it very quietly in the name of a company called Voyager Properties."

"Using money she took from her Voyagers, I assume?"

"Probably. But there's nothing illegal about her firm as far as we can tell. She's the president. Only one employee on the payroll."

"Let me guess. Rick Swinton?"

"Actually, his full name is Richard Swinton. Sounds like you've made his acquaintance."

"He paid me a visit last night. Uninvited."

"I see," Craig said. "Want me to dig deeper into his background?"

"I'll probably ask for more information after I repay Swinton's visit."

"Sounds like the two of you are getting friendly."

"You know how it is in a small town. Everyone tries to be neighborly."

"Better pay your return visit before this Swinton character leaves on a spaceship," Craig said.

"I'll do that."

"By the way, I have some unrelated news that may be of interest to you."

Elias gazed at Otis through the office doorway. The

bird was sidling impatiently back and forth along his perch. It was closing time. "What news?"

"Remember Garrick Keyworth? The guy you had me do some work on?"

Elias went still. "What about him?"

"Word has it that he tried to commit suicide last night. Took a whole fistful of pills."

All of the air went out of Elias's lungs. With no warning, the river that flowed out of his own past suddenly revealed the pale form of his mother. She lay sprawled on a bed, an array of pill bottles neatly arranged on the night table beside her.

With an act of practiced will, Elias sent the image back into the darkness from which it had come.

"Did he succeed?" Elias asked.

"No. Nine-one-one was called. They got him to the hospital in time. He'll recover, but you can imagine what the news will do to the company. Once the shock wears off, Keyworth International is expected to go into a tailspin. You know how it is in an operation like that where there's no clear successor poised to take over the leadership slot. Everyone panics."

"Yes."

"Too bad Keyworth never took his son into the firm. If he had, there would be someone at the helm now to calm customers and creditors."

"Keyworth and his son are estranged," Elias said.

"So I heard. Well, I'd say this will be the end of Keyworth International."

7

A man can drown in passion as surely as he can drown in the sea.

—"On the Way of Water," from the journal of Hayden Stone

Something was wrong.

Charity closed the new issue of *Gourmet,* which she had been poring over for the past half hour. She could feel the wrongness in her bones. The feeling of unease had been growing steadily since late this afternoon when she had seen Elias lock up his shop for the night.

He hadn't even bothered to wave good-bye to anyone, let alone see Charity to her car, as had become his habit during the past few days. He had set off toward the parking lot without a backward glance, empty travel cage in one hand. Otis had perched like a vulture on his shoulder.

For some inexplicable reason, the sight of man and bird pacing down the pier had sent a chill through

Charity. Now, several hours later, the cold feeling was getting worse.

She tossed the glossy magazine onto the whimsically designed, frosted-glass coffee table. It landed on a bevy of cookbooks that she had brought home from Whispers. She had spent the entire evening scouring the collection for interesting recipes. Elias's tastes, like hers, were distinctive and a little eccentric. Nothing had been said aloud, but Charity sensed that a gauntlet had been thrown down. Elias had deliberately challenged her. She intended to hold her own in the next round of the Truitt-Winters cook-off.

But what she was feeling now was not a form of chef's anxiety. This restlessness was different.

She could not get the image of Elias's grim silhouette against the evening sun out of her mind.

Something was definitely wrong.

She uncurled from the curved lipstick-red sofa and walked across the small living room to open the front door. She stepped out onto the porch. It was after nine. Nearly full dark. There was a new chill in the air. Fog was gathering over the cove.

She curled her hands around the old, white-washed rail and studied the maze of trees that stretched the quarter-mile distance that separated her cottage from Elias's. She could not make out any sign of light through the thick foliage.

On impulse she straightened, locked the front door, and went down the porch steps. She paused again, listening to the sounds of the onrushing night. She thought she could hear the distant chants of the Voyagers, but it was difficult to tell for certain.

She walked out to the bluff path. Once again she gazed in the direction of Elias's cottage. From here she should be able to see lights from his windows through the trees.

Nothing. Not so much as a glimmer from his porch light. Perhaps he had gone into town for the evening.

The sense of wrongness grew stronger.

She took one step and then another along the path. She had covered several yards before she acknowledged that she was going to walk to Elias's cottage.

This was probably a mistake. Checking up on Elias could prove to be an embarrassing move in the cat-and-mouse flirtation game that the two of them seemed to be playing. He'd probably view her curiosity as a sign of eagerness or even desperation. She would lose the upper hand.

But she could not make herself turn back.

What the hell. She never had been any good at the kind of games men and women played. There had never been any time to practice.

The night closed swiftly in around her as she hurried along the top of the bluffs. When she reached Elias's madrona-shaded garden she saw that there was still no light in the windows. She walked around to the front of the cottage. Elias's Jeep was parked in the drive.

She wondered if he had gone for an evening walk farther up along the bluffs.

Charity made her way back around the cottage to the garden entrance. For a moment she stood, one hand resting on the low gate. After a moment she raised the latch and went into the garden.

She was halfway along the winding path, headed toward the unlit porch, when she sensed another presence in the garden. She stopped and turned slowly.

It took a few seconds for her to make out Elias. He sat cross-legged in front of the reflecting pool, a still, silent figure shrouded in twilight shadows. The small pond was a black mirror that revealed nothing.

"Elias?" She took a step forward and hesitated.

"Was there something you wanted?" His voice held the distant, chillingly detached quality that had unnerved her on the day they had met.

"No." She took another step toward him. "Are you all right?"

"Yes."

"Elias, for heaven's sake, what's wrong?"

"An interesting aspect of water is only revealed when there is an absence of light. The surface becomes as opaque to the eye as a wall of obsidian."

"Great, we're back to the Zen-speak." Charity walked to the edge of the pond and halted a short distance from Elias. "Enough with the cryptic comments. Tell me what's going on here."

At first she thought that he would not respond. He did not move, did not even look at her. He seemed completely focused on the dark, blank surface of the reflecting pool. An endless moment passed.

"Garrick Keyworth tried to commit suicide last night," he said at last.

The stark words hit her with the force of a wave crashing on rocks. She recalled what Elias had said about his mother's death. Suicide always held a special horror for those who had been touched by it.

"Oh, Elias."

She sank down beside him. A section of the hem of her light chambray dress settled on his knee. She followed his gaze into the darkness of the reflecting pool. He was right. There was nothing to be seen there. The night sat heavily on the garden.

Time passed. Charity did not attempt to break the silence. She simply waited. It was the only thing she could do.

"I thought that because I had decided to walk away from my revenge, the matter was finished," Elias said after a while. "But I did not truly turn aside. I went to Keyworth one last time. Showed him what I could have done to him, had I chosen to go through with it."

"You don't know that your meeting with him had anything to do with his suicide attempt."

"It had everything to do with it. I studied him for years. I should have seen the full range of possibilities when I made my last move. Maybe I did see them but refused to acknowledge them."

"Don't be so hard on yourself, Elias."

"I knew damn well that the knowledge of his own vulnerability would add to the poison brewing inside Keyworth. But I told myself that it would be only a single small drop in the mixture. Not enough to change the final results."

"You couldn't have known that it would push him over the edge. You still don't know that it did."

"It takes only a small impurity to destroy the perfection of the clearest pond."

Charity tried to think of something to say, but everything that came to mind was useless. A less self-aware, less self-disciplined man might have been comforted by her insistence that he was not responsible for Keyworth's suicide attempt. A less complicated man might have taken triumphant satisfaction from the situation. After all, some would say that had Keyworth been successful, it would have been nothing more than simple justice. But Elias was not like most men. Elias was different.

After a while Charity reached out to touch his arm. Every muscle, every tendon, every sinew beneath his skin was as taut as twisted steel. He did not move. He seemed oblivious to her fingers.

"It's getting chilly out here," she said eventually. "Come inside. I'll fix you some tea."

"I don't want any tea. Go home, Charity."

The icy remoteness in his voice made her want to

recoil. She fought the instinctive urge to leap to her feet and run. "I'm not going to leave you sitting out here. There's a fog bank moving in over the cove, in case you haven't noticed. The temperature is dropping."

"I can take care of myself. I don't need your help. Leave me alone, Charity. You shouldn't have come here tonight."

"We're neighbors, remember? Friends. I can't leave you alone."

"You have no responsibility for me."

"Listen up, Mr. Control Freak, you've got your code, and I've got mine. Mine says I can't leave you out here by yourself." She got to her feet and tugged on his arm. "Please, Elias. Let's go inside."

He looked up at her with eyes as unreadable as the surface of the reflecting pool. For a moment she thought he would refuse. Then, without a word he rose to his feet in a single, fluid movement.

She took advantage of the small victory to lead him up the steps. He did not resist, but the hard tension in him did not ease. She opened the door and urged him gently inside.

She kicked off her shoes and groped along the wall. "Where's the light switch?"

Without a word, Elias extended one hand and flipped a switch. A lamp glowed in the corner. Otis muttered a complaint from beneath the cover that encircled his cage.

For the first time Charity got a clear look at Elias's face. What she saw there made her wish she hadn't asked him to turn on the light. Some things were best left concealed in the shadows.

On the other hand, some things only got more scary if they were hidden in the dark.

"I'll put the water on," she said.

"I think you'd better leave, Charity. I'm not going to be good company tonight."

The words were an unmistakable warning. A tiny frisson of fear went through her. She shook off the sense of impending danger. "I said I'd fix you a cup of tea."

She brushed past him and crossed the barren room to the small kitchen. The kettle sat on a back burner. She discovered a pot in a cupboard. There was a cannister of Kemun beside it.

"I doubt if my tea will be up to your standards, but at least it will be hot." She ran water into the kettle.

"Charity."

She paused, kettle in hand, and glanced at him over her shoulder.

"Yes?"

He said nothing. He simply stood there, watching her with a shattering intensity that paralyzed her. She was riveted by the bleakness in his gaze. In that moment she could see straight through the wall of pride and self-discipline he had so painstakingly built around himself. An ancient loneliness crouched like some great monstrous beast in the darkness beyond the wall.

"Elias," she said very softly. Slowly she put down the kettle. "I know you think you can handle this by yourself, and you're probably right. But sometimes it's better not to try to go it alone. That stuff about the Way of Water may work just fine as a philosophical construct, but sometimes a person needs more."

"Tal Kek Chara is all I have," he said with stark simplicity.

"That's not true." She shook off the spell that had seized her and went to him.

She put her arms around him and hugged him with fierce determination. He was hard and unyielding.

Aware that she was engaged in a battle of unknown dimensions, she tightened her arms and pressed her face against his shoulder. With a sense of desperation, she willed her warmth and something more, something she was not certain she wanted to identify, into the center of his being.

A shudder went through Elias. With a low, hoarse groan, he captured her head between his hands.

"You should have gone home," he said.

And then his mouth was on hers. The beast of loneliness howled.

Charity swayed beneath the onslaught of a masculine hunger that threatened to drown her. For a moment, everything threatened to disappear.

When the mist cleared slightly, she realized that she was in Elias's arms. He had picked her up and was carrying her toward the dark opening that marked the doorway of the bedroom.

She felt herself being lowered onto a cushion of some sort. It had to be a futon, she thought. Nothing else would be this hard and uncomfortable. The man slept on a *futon*. That was taking self-discipline a little too far.

But she had no time to complain. He came down on top of her and she promptly forgot about the overly firm bedding. Elias was far more rigid than his futon.

His lean, powerful body was a sexy weight crushing her into the dense cushions. The kiss was endlessly deep, infinitely mysterious, not unlike Elias himself.

Charity wrapped her arms around his neck. His fingers went to the buttons of her loose, chambray dress. She heard him inhale sharply when he uncovered her breasts. His palm closed over one nipple, and it was her turn to gasp. She felt herself tighten at his touch. Another savage shudder went through him.

"You shouldn't have come here tonight," he muttered.

"It's all right, Elias." Her head fell back across his arm. One of his legs slid between her thighs. He pushed his knee upward, shoving aside the skirt of her dress. The denim of his jeans was rough and strangely exciting against her bare skin.

"You shouldn't be here, but I can't send you away now. God help me, I want you too much."

He pulled free of her mouth and bent his head to catch the crown of her breast between his teeth. His hand went to the rapidly dampening crotch of her panties. He squeezed gently, urgently. One strong finger eased beneath the elastic edge. He tugged off the undergarment in a single, swift movement.

A driving excitement washed over Charity, a giant wave that gathered her up and tumbled her about until she was dazed and disoriented. She had never felt so gloriously wild in her life. She yanked Elias's shirt free of his jeans and sank her fingers into his sleekly contoured back.

For some reason, it came as a shock to discover how warm he was. She sensed the muscles working smoothly, powerfully beneath his skin. The tang of his scent was electrifyingly male.

She fumbled with the pliant strip of leather that he wore outside the belt loops of his jeans. There was no buckle. She could not figure out how to unfasten the odd knot. In mounting frustration, she jerked at a trailing end.

"I'll take care of it." He levered himself away from her long enough to remove the unusual belt.

The knot that had proved so stubborn beneath her fingers, came undone at a single touch of his hand. He shifted again to toss the length of leather down beside the futon. She heard the slide of a metal zipper.

He rolled to one side, pulled off his jeans, and reached into the open chest beside the futon. Charity heard the distinctive sound of tearing foil. Elias's hands moved deftly.

A moment later he rolled back on top of her. She tensed when she felt the broad head of his sheathed erection pressing against her damp body. He was heavy and thick.

Big. Definitely big. But it was excitement she felt, not panic.

He centered himself between her legs. "Look at me."

She opened her eyes, responding instantly to the urgency in his words. There was just enough light filtering in from the front room to allow her to see the stark hunger in him. The rush of her own response made her tremble.

She drove her fingers through his hair. "I want you, Elias."

"No more games," he whispered.

"No more games."

He thrust into her in a slow, endless motion that shocked all of her senses. Everything within her froze. She could not think, could not speak, could not move. He filled her completely. Stretched her to the point of pain. Every muscle in her body was coiled spring-tight in response to the sensual invasion.

Locked deep inside her, Elias went as still as everything else in the universe. He stared down at her as if waiting for some signal to finish what had been begun.

"Are you all right?" he asked in a voice that shook a little around the edges.

Charity took a deep breath and rediscovered her own tongue. "Yes. Yes, I'm very much all right." She clenched her fingers tightly in his hair and lifted herself cautiously against him.

A husky groan vibrated deep in his chest. "I don't want to hurt you. You're so small and tight. I didn't realize—"

"I said, it's all right." She smiled up at him.

"My God, Charity." He bent his head and kissed the curve of her shoulder.

The unbearable tightness eased. The world began to revolve once more.

Elias retreated slowly, cautiously and then pushed steadily back into her. This time excitement accompanied the overwhelming sense of fullness. Charity sighed hungrily and dug her nails into his shoulders.

He responded with a swift intake of breath. One of his hands slid down her body to the point where they were joined. He found the exquisitely sensitive nub in the nest of crisp, curling hair and stroked deliberately.

Electricity shot through her. She arched and cried out.

"So good," he whispered. "So real."

She swallowed a wild urge to laugh. "Of course I'm real. What did you think I was? Just another reflection on the water?"

"I wasn't quite certain until now."

He stroked again and again and all the seething tension within her exploded in wave after wave of release. She felt his teeth on her earlobe as he drove into her one last time.

His body stiffened in climax. His hoarse, soundless cry echoed in the darkness.

Charity let the night take her.

No more games.

Elias opened his eyes and looked at the dark ceiling. The scent of spent passion mingled with the cool fog-laced air that came through the partially opened window. He was acutely aware of the warm curve of Charity's thigh pressed against his leg.

He could feel the satisfaction in every quadrant of his body. It sang in his veins and created a pleasant warmth in his belly. He stretched, languid and relaxed and content.

No more games.

It felt good.

It felt dangerous.

Control was everything in Tal Kek Chara. To lose control was to be swept away by the raging tide into the deepest part of the sea. To lose control was to be caught up in the churning rapids of a primeval river. To lose control was to go over the falls, to plummet down through the depths of an icy-cold, bottomless lake.

To lose control was to lose everything.

The following morning Charity gazed out the window at the fog that had enveloped Whispering Waters Cove during the night. "If this doesn't lift by tonight, the spaceships may not get clearance to land."

"Something tells me it won't make much difference," Elias said. "Ready for breakfast?"

"Sure." She turned away from the window. "But I hope you kept it simple. It's okay to show off at dinner, but it's not fair when it comes to breakfast. Breakfast is not a competitive sport."

Elias's brows rose as he set two bowls on the low table. "Think of it as a challenge."

She summoned what she hoped was a breezy, sophisticated smile as she sank down onto one of the cushions in front of the table. "Push me too far, and I'll throw in the towel and send out for pizza tonight."

"No, you won't. That would be the coward's way, and you're no coward." He sat down across from her

JAYNE ANN KRENTZ

and poured tea from the brown, earthenware pot. "I'm sure you'll rise to the occasion. Something tells me you always do."

"I hate to disappoint you, but I lost a lot of my competitive edge when I quit the corporate world."

The attempt at casual conversation took an extraordinary amount of effort. Charity was not in a light-hearted mood. The uncertainty that gripped her this morning came as a complete surprise. This was not how she had expected to feel after last night's intense lovemaking. It made her uncomfortable. There was no panic yet, but she could definitely hear alarm bells.

This subtle tension between herself and Elias was not right. Not the way things should be today.

Where was the sense of intimacy that ought to have enveloped both of them in a warm cocoon this morning? she wondered. Only hours ago she had felt incredibly close to Elias. Now there was a disturbing distance between them.

She was all too well aware that her experience of sex was not what anyone would call extensive, and it was several years out of date. Her responsibilities to Truitt had imprisoned her in an artificial cloister for years. This was, in fact, the first time that she had ever actually stayed the night with a man and shared breakfast with him the next morning. Nevertheless, her instincts told her that it shouldn't be like this between the two of them.

Something very special had happened between them last night. Elias had let her see a piece of his soul.

But things were all wrong today. He was back in his remote, self-contained universe. She could not touch him the way she had touched him last night.

He had said that there would be no more games, but this morning she felt as if they were both back out on the playing field.

She stifled a small sigh and looked down at the interesting concoction in her bowl. "What is this?"

"Muesli. My own recipe. Oats, rye, sesame seeds, almonds, dried fruit, yogurt, and a touch of vanilla and honey."

"So much for keeping breakfast noncompetitive." She added milk to the muesli and picked up a spoon.

"When I stay the night with you, I'll fix breakfast," he offered with suspicious generosity.

Charity coughed and nearly choked on a bite of cereal. She put down her spoon and grabbed the small teacup.

"Are you okay?" Elias asked.

She nodded quickly and swallowed tea to clear her throat. "Fine. Just fine. Sesame seed went down the wrong way."

He regarded her with a long, steady gaze. "Does the thought of me spending the night in your bed make you nervous?"

"Of course not." She gulped more hot tea. "Don't be ridiculous." With a heroic effort she summoned a confident smile. "But I'm sure neither one of us wants to rush things. We'll take our time. Let the relationship develop naturally."

His eyes narrowed faintly. "I thought we agreed last night that there would be no more games."

She felt the heat rise in her cheeks. "Letting a relationship mature and develop at its own pace is not considered game-playing. It's just common sense."

"What's wrong, Charity?"

"Nothing's wrong." She let the smile drop. "I'm just trying to sort things out, that's all."

"What's to sort out?"

Anger flared out of nowhere. "You have to ask me that?" She set the teacup down so hard that it threatened to crack. Otis grumbled at the noise. "You're the one who's been acting as if nothing out of the ordinary happened last night."

He gazed at her for a long while. "About last night."

She held up a hand. "Please. If this is the part where you tell me not to read too much into what happened between us last night, forget it. I'm trying to eat my breakfast. You can give me the lecture later."

"No."

"You want to go back to playing games, fine. Go play with yourself."

"That idea lacks a certain appeal," he said dryly. "Especially after last night."

She felt herself turn red. "You know what I mean."

"Yes. But I don't think you understand what I'm trying to say here."

"Hah. That's what you think. I understand exactly what you're trying to say." She tapped her spoon on the edge of the bowl. "You want to tell me that you weren't yourself last night, don't you? That I shouldn't assume too much because of what happened. That you're sorry we spent the night together."

He hesitated. "You've got it half right. I wasn't in a good place last night."

"Uh-huh." She stabbed her spoon into the muesli.

"I wasn't expecting you to show up. I had a lot of thinking to do."

"And I interrupted you?"

"To be blunt, yes, you did. It would have been better if you had not come into the garden when you did."

"Sorry about that." She spooned up a mouthful of muesli and chewed with a vengeance. "Won't happen again."

He frowned. "You don't get it."

"Sure, I do. I'm an ex-CEO, remember? I can boil

down even the most complicated issues into simple concepts. Problem? You wish I hadn't shown up last night. Solution? Simple. We'll just pretend it never happened."

"That's not going to be possible."

She smiled grimly. "Watch me."

"You're angry."

She thought about it. "Yeah, you could say that."

"Charity, I'm trying to get something clear between us."

"Maybe it would be better if you just ate your breakfast instead."

He ignored that. "What I'm trying to tell you is that I regret that you interrupted me while I was in the middle of a contemplation session last night. I was trying to sort out some things. I think that you might have drawn some false conclusions based on what happened after you showed up."

She halted the spoon halfway to her mouth, as realization dawned. "Wait a second. I think I'm getting a glimmer here."

"Let's just say that it would not be wise for you to assume that my actions last night indicated that I was—" He broke off, frowning.

"Weak? Normal?" She paused delicately. "Human?"

A dark flush stained his fierce cheekbones. "I don't want you to get the wrong impression, that's all."

"Elias, think of this in terms of your water philosophy. You can't stay in the shallow end of the pool all of your life, thinking you'll be safe. Sometimes you just have to take a chance and jump in at the deep end."

"That analogy is not an appropriate application of the philosophical principles of Tal Kek Chara," he said through his teeth. "The Way is a method of seeing clearly. A guide to observing reality."

"But you're not an observer. You're a participant. At least you were last night."

"You're missing the point here."

She leveled her spoon at him. "Okay, enlighten me, oh, great Master of Tal Kek Chara. Take a look into your magic reflecting pool and tell me what you see happening between us right now at this very moment."

"That's exactly what I'm trying to do," he said swiftly. "I don't want you to be under any misconceptions about me. I realize that my behavior last night may have given you the impression that I allowed Keyworth's attempt at suicide to get to me."

"Didn't it?"

"His attempt to take his own life was an unforeseen consequence of my actions." A harsh, bleak acceptance burned in Elias's eyes. "And I don't like it when unforeseen consequences occur. It means that I failed to use Tal Kek Chara correctly."

"Hey, nobody's perfect."

"That is no excuse," he shot back.

"Elias, it's not your fault that Keyworth tried to commit suicide. But if it's going to eat at you like this, I suggest you do something about it."

"Such as?"

She hesitated, thinking quickly. "You could go see him, I suppose. That would be a start. Talk to him. Make your peace with him."

"And just how the hell do you suggest that I do that, Madam Therapist? What am I supposed to say to a man who tried to kill himself because of me?"

"I don't know. I've never been in a situation like this. Maybe you need to tell him that you don't want the past to repeat itself. Does he have children?"

"A son who hates his guts."

Charity nodded. "Tell Keyworth not to do to his kid what your parents did to you."

"My parents." Elias looked thunderstruck.

"Tell Keyworth he's got no right to abandon his son. That if he really wants to atone for what happened all those years ago on Nihili, he must fulfill his responsibilities in the present."

Elias stared at her. Charity could almost see him gathering himself, searching for the center, summoning his power. She thought she caught another fleeting glimpse of the beast of loneliness prowling within him just before the barriers solidified and shut her out.

"You don't know enough about the situation to make a suggestion like that," Elias said in a voice that was more remote than the moon. "Forget about Keyworth. I'll deal with it."

"Sure."

"About us," he began deliberately. "I told you a few minutes ago that you were half right when you said that I regret that you came into my garden last night and that we spent the night together."

"I think I can guess which half I got right. You wish I hadn't seen you acting like a normal human being with your defenses down, but, what the hell, the sex was okay."

"The sex was a lot better than okay."

She managed a cool smile. "Yes, it was, wasn't it?"

He pushed his uneaten muesli aside and folded his arms on the low table. "It might have been better if we had waited to begin our relationship under more auspicious circumstances. But what's done is done."

"That's certainly a charmingly romantic view of our little night of passion."

"What I'm trying to say is that, while I wish it had

happened at a different time, I don't regret that we've moved to the next stage of our relationship."

Charity looked at her watch. "Good grief, it's nearly eight o'clock. I've got to run home, change, and get ready to open the shop at ten."

"Charity—"

"I'll see you at the pier." She leaped to her feet, scooped up her bowl and spoon, and dashed across the room to dump them into the sink.

"Damn it, Charity, wait a minute."

"Don't forget, dinner at my place this evening." She stepped into her sandals and yanked open the front door. "This is the big night for the Voyagers and their spaceships. Better bring a jacket. It'll probably be chilly out on the bluff at midnight."

She fled into the early-morning fog.

8

The currents shift without warning yet the surface of the water appears to be the same to the observer. In such a situation there is great danger.

—"On the Way of Water," from the journal of Hayden Stone

Charity pounced on the perfectly shaped red bell pepper in the grocery store vegetable bin. "Gotcha."

She slipped several more plump peppers into a plastic bag and placed her booty in the shopping cart.

Seizing the handlebar of the cart, she leaned into the task of forcing it down another aisle. It took considerable effort to keep the vehicle tracking in a reasonably straight line. One wheel kept veering off at a crazy angle.

She breathed a sigh of relief when she found the packages of dried seaweed next to the seasoned rice wine vinegar. She grabbed two envelopes full of the glistening, dark green sheets of *nori* and a bottle of the vinegar and dumped it all into the cart.

It hadn't been easy selecting a menu for tonight's dinner. Her main concern had been choosing recipes that called for ingredients she could count on finding at the Whispering Waters Cove Grocery. A year ago when she first moved into town, tonight's menu would have been an impossible dream. But her intensive efforts to cultivate the store manager had paid off.

The real problem, she decided as she did battle with the recalcitrant cart, was not locating the ingredients for tonight's dinner. The more critical issue was, why was she bothering to cook a meal for Elias Winters in the first place?

She was still simmering over their early-morning conversation. He had made it breathtakingly clear that he wanted to pretend that he had never shown her that vulnerable piece of himself last night. On the other hand, he was content to carry on with the sexual side of their relationship now that it had gotten off the ground.

Typical, Charity thought. It was just so damn typical.

No, that wasn't fair, she decided as she reached for a package of rice and some soy sauce. Nothing about Elias could be called typical.

She glanced at her list. She still needed fresh fruit for the dessert. It was getting late. She had left Newlin in charge of closing Whispers while she took off to do her grocery shopping, but she still had a number of things to do before Elias arrived on her doorstep.

She muscled the grocery cart around a corner and saw another cart blocking her path. Jennifer Pitt had the door of the frozen food case open.

"Oops, sorry, Jennifer." For some reason, Charity's cart, which until now had fought her every inch of the way, suddenly took off like a thoroughbred racehorse.

Charity dug in her heels and managed to drag it to a halt. "Didn't see you."

Jennifer smiled her cool, bored smile. "Don't worry about it. These aisles are far too narrow. When things start to boom here in the Cove, I'd like to see a major grocery chain move into town. We could certainly use a decent store here."

"This one's not so bad. Just a little small."

"You could say that about the whole damn town."

Charity started to back out of the aisle. The last thing she wanted to do was get into an extended conversation with the second Mrs. Pitt. Jennifer was not a happy woman. Of course, it had not been an easy summer for her, what with the flamboyant first Mrs. Pitt flitting around town in her outrageous Voyager costume.

In Charity's opinion, Jennifer had actually handled the whole thing with surprising grace. Perhaps the knowledge that she was the current Mrs. Pitt, not the ex, gave her the fortitude to rise above the awkward situation.

Jennifer was a tall, sleek, striking woman in her mid-thirties. Rumor had it that she had once done a short stint as a model in Los Angeles. Charity could well believe it. She had the height, and there was a certain kind of Southern California glamour about her. It whispered of hot beaches and endless summers. Everyone knew she worked out regularly on the home gym equipment Leighton had purchased for her. The results showed.

She had a sense of fashion that was alien to Whispering Waters Cove. Today she wore a silk shirt designed to imitate denim and a pair of beautifully draped trousers that flowed over the cuffs of her shoes.

Her honey-brown mane was streaked with a lot of

golden highlights, as if she lived in perpetual sunshine instead of in the cloudy Northwest. She wore her big hair in a voluminous, shoulder-length style that always managed to look just slightly windblown. The large diamond that Leighton had given her on their wedding day glittered on her left hand. She always had a pair of stylish dark glasses perched on top of her head, and her makeup was flawless.

Most folks held the view that Leighton Pitt had never stood a chance once Jennifer set her sights on him. The biggest mystery in Whispering Waters Cove was not why he had divorced Gwendolyn to marry Jennifer. The mystery was why Jennifer had ever wanted to steal him in the first place.

True, Leighton was the most prosperous man in the Cove, but most people felt that, with her looks and style, Jennifer could have done much better for herself in Seattle. After all there was *real* money in the city, everyone pointed out, what with all the high-tech companies and the Pacific Rim businesses located there.

"I suppose you'll be joining the crowd on the bluff at midnight tonight." Jennifer's long, red-tipped acrylic nails closed around a ready-made, low-fat entrée.

"Wouldn't miss it." Charity glanced curiously at the microwavable meal Jennifer had selected. It was a single-serving size. "Biggest show in town."

"Which isn't saying much, is it?" Jennifer's crimson mouth twisted with just a hint of bitterness as she closed the freezer door. "Well, at least it will all be over by tomorrow. Gwendolyn's Voyagers will finally realize that they've been had. Wonder what they'll do about it when they find out they've been ripped off?"

Charity thought about it. "I suppose some of them might sue."

Jennifer lifted one shoulder in an elegant little shrug. "I doubt if that would do any good. I'm sure

Gwendolyn and her friend, Rick Swinton, have made
certain that the money is well protected."

"Maybe nothing much will change after the spaceships fail to arrive," Charity suggested. "A friend of
mine says that people who want to believe in something will often go on believing in it even in the face
of overwhelming proof that it doesn't exist."

"Your friend may be right." Jennifer's gaze shifted
to a point just beyond Charity's right shoulder. Her eyes
narrowed. "Some people who turned over their savings
to a swindler might prefer to continue to believe rather
than to admit they'd been conned. But others might get
a little pissed when they discover the truth."

Without waiting for a response, she twirled her
shopping cart around with a single-handed grip on the
handlebar. The cart obeyed instantly. It never even
wobbled. Under Jennifer's guidance, it maneuvered
down the aisle with the pinpoint precision of a fine
European sports car.

Charity watched in admiration. Some people had all
the luck when it came to selecting shopping carts.

"My, my. Little Miss California seems to be in a
snit today," Gwendolyn Pitt drawled behind Charity.
"And you can bet she isn't feeding that low-fat frozen
dinner to Leighton. Oh, no. I expect that he'll be clog-
ging up his arteries with beer and nachos down at the
Cove Tavern again tonight. Sweet Jennifer is probably
hoping that he'll conveniently drop dead from a
heart attack."

Charity turned reluctantly. Gwendolyn was in full
Voyager regalia. Her long blue and white robes
looked even more bizarre than usual against the mundane backdrop of a small-town grocery store.

The guru look was an interesting contrast to the
shrewd, assessing expression in Gwendolyn's eyes.
Charity was fairly certain she could still see signs of

the successful real estate broker beneath the exotic attire.

"Hello, Gwendolyn. Ready for the big night?"

"Of course. All the Voyagers are ready. We have been preparing ourselves for this night for months." Gwendolyn watched Jennifer disappear around the corner of the aisle, and then she switched her sharp gaze to Charity. "I'm sure everyone in town will find it fascinating."

"You can bet we'll all be there on the bluff." Charity grabbed hold of her cart handle and prepared to escape. "Of course, if this fog doesn't lift, we might not be able to see the starships arrive."

"Don't worry," Gwendolyn murmured. "The entire town will find out soon enough that something interesting has happened."

Nothing yields so easily as water, yet nothing is so powerful. He who seeks to follow the Way must first acknowledge his own strengths and weaknesses.

Hayden Stone's advice burned in Elias's mind as he whirled through the last movement of the twisting, gliding pattern. He breathed out and allowed the leather belt to seek its target. The end of the belt struck with the speed and accuracy of a snake. It wrapped itself around the empty aluminum pop can and crushed it.

Elias drew a deep breath and bent down to pick up the crumpled can. Not good. He had used too much force. His control was not what it should have been today.

He walked to the edge of the bluff and looked out over the fog-shrouded cove.

His timing and calculation had been off during the entire practice session, and it didn't take an hour's contemplation on the Way of Water to figure out why.

Memories of last night kept getting in the way of his concentration.

Elias gazed into the gray mist as the images crashed through his head.

Charity sitting down beside him at the edge of the reflecting pool.

Charity sliding her fingers through his hair as she offered him her mouth.

Charity looking into his eyes and knowing what the news of Keyworth's suicide attempt had done to him.

Charity trembling with passion as she lay beneath him.

He'd been wrong about one thing. There had been no problem making love to Charity on the futon. He could have made love to her on the floor or the beach or anywhere else, for that matter. The thing that worried him the most at the moment was not knowing when he would be able to make love to her again.

The hot need simmered inside him. Last night had only whetted his appetite. Today, instead of satisfaction, there was only a deeper hunger.

They had agreed that there would be no more games between them. But this morning she had made it clear that she was still prepared to play them. He knew why she had shied away from a full commitment to the affair they had begun during the night. It was as Hayden Stone had warned him years ago. A woman worth wanting always demanded a great deal in return.

Elias knew that Charity wanted more than just good sex. She wanted his soul. She wanted to assure herself that she had true power over him.

He became aware of the cooling perspiration on his bare shoulders. The elaborate movements of Tal Kek Chara had done little to alleviate the tension he had been feeling all day.

He was still aware of the edgy feeling later that evening when he found himself in Charity's kitchen. Elias saw right away that they were both going to play it cool. She was no longer intense and emotional the way she had been this morning when she had left his cottage. They were back to the easy flirtation that had characterized their relationship for the past several days.

Just two friendly people involved in an affair. That was good, he assured himself. He wondered irritably why he did not feel incredibly relieved by the deliberately diminished tides of intensity.

He lounged in the doorway of Charity's kitchen and surveyed the wonderland of gleaming pans, Euro-style appliances, and high-tech gadgets. The kitchen matched the rest of the cottage, which was crammed with the sophisticated furnishings Charity had brought with her when she moved to the cove.

It was all a far cry from the stark simplicity of his own place, Elias thought. But it was oddly pleasant to watch Charity work amid her sleek, colorful surroundings.

Absently he swirled the chardonnay in his glass. "I didn't get a chance to tell you what my lawyer, Craig Thorgood, learned about Gwendolyn Pitt and her Voyagers."

Charity shot him a surprised glance over her shoulder before she resumed whisking soy sauce, ginger, lime juice, and sherry in a bowl. "Anything interesting?"

"Nothing startling. Just the guru business as usual. Gwendolyn has created a company called Voyager Investments. She's the president, and Swinton is her sole employee."

Charity paused again in her whisking and looked thoughtful. "Then the money they've taken from the cult members is out there somewhere. It might be traceable."

Elias smiled faintly. "I think it's a safe bet that it's very traceable. I'm sure Gwendolyn and Swinton have it under close surveillance."

"Maybe some of the Voyagers can get it back after the spaceships fail to show up tonight. I have a feeling Arlene Fenton, for one, is going to be in desperate straits once she realizes she's not bound for the stars. Newlin says she turned over everything in her bank account to the Voyagers organization."

"It wouldn't be easy to retrieve anyone's assets without the cooperation of Pitt or Swinton. And I doubt if either of them will be inclined to cooperate."

"They probably plan to take the money and run," Charity agreed. "Although Gwendolyn Pitt said something strange today in the grocery store."

"What was that?"

"Something about the entire town finding out soon that something interesting had happened tonight."

"I don't doubt it. The only question is, why is today's date so important to her?" Elias caught the fragrance of the ginger and inhaled appreciatively. "Are you going to tell me what's on the menu?"

"Vegetable sushi, roasted red pepper salad, and a nectarine and blueberry tart."

"I don't believe it. You talked the store manager into stocking *nori?*"

Charity smiled. "I didn't spend all those years running Truitt for nothing. I've had plenty of experience in the art of the deal."

"I can see that the competition is heating up. This could get ugly. Or maybe I should say tasty."

"I'm sure you'll think of something amusingly unpretentious yet elegant when it's your turn to cook. I can see you doing a dish of stunning simplicity that is infused with flavors that retain their integrity even as they enhance the other elements involved."

"Let me guess. You've been reading food magazines, haven't you?"

"Yep." She dropped the whisk into the sink. "I also saw the second Mrs. Pitt in the grocery store this afternoon. A touch of animosity between the first and the second. I was lucky I didn't get crushed between their shopping carts."

"Not surprising."

"No."

Elias sipped his wine. "I've got to admit, I'm getting a little curious about Gwendolyn's plans."

"Join the crowd."

"But I'm even more curious about Rick Swinton."

"Why the special interest in him?"

"Because he's interested in me."

Charity paused, cocked a brow, and gave him a look. "Funny. I wouldn't have said that you were each other's type."

"I used the word in the other sense. Apparently Swinton has some questions about me. He searched my house on Friday night."

"He *what?*" Charity whirled around, her eyes huge. "You're joking. He went through your things? How do you know?"

"I got a pretty big clue when I stood in my garden and watched him crawl out of my house through the front window."

"Good lord." Charity put down the small bowl, turned her back to the counter, and braced herself against the tiled edge. "That's incredible. I can hardly believe it."

"He seemed a little nervous, but I got the impression it wasn't the first time he'd entertained himself with an evening of B and E. After he finished at my house, he went down to Charms & Virtues and took a look around."

"That's outrageous. Absolutely outrageous. Did he take anything?"

"No."

"Did you call Chief Tybern?"

"No."

She spread her hands. "But what he did was illegal. You can't just ignore it."

"I figure Swinton and I will be even in the breaking and entering category after tonight."

"Wait a second. You don't mean that you plan to . . . to—"

"Search his motor home while everyone's watching the show down on the beach?" Elias swallowed the last of his wine. "Yes. That's exactly what I plan to do."

Charity decided that the scene on the bluff at eleven-thirty that night was a cross between a low-budget horror film and a carnival. The special effects consisted primarily of fog. The thick stuff blanketed the waters of the cove and swirled around the herd of vehicles occupied by the sightseers from town.

The Voyagers' RVs and trailers loomed in the mist. The weak lamps above the entrance to the campground rest rooms glowed bravely, but the light did not penetrate far.

From what Charity could discover, the Voyagers were all down on the beach. She could hear their hypnotic chants rising and falling above the sound of the gentle waves. The flute player was still off-key, she noticed. The drummer was trying to compensate with volume. The fog reflected an eerie glow created by flashlights and camp lanterns.

Charity glanced back over her shoulder at the array

of cars and trucks parked along the bluff. Most of the town had turned out to see the Voyagers off on their trip through the galaxy. Many adults waited inside their vehicles or visited with friends. A few men had gathered near the entrance to the primary bluff path They were drinking beer and roaring with laughter. Dozens of small children dashed about playing tag in front of the first row of parked cars.

The teenage contingent had braved the chill and the fog to cluster near the fence that overlooked the beach. Their shouts and jokes mingled with the serious chants of the Voyagers. Several drank cans of soda that they had purchased from the tailgate refreshment stand Bea and Yappy had set up.

Radiance had joined the teenagers to hang over the railing. Ted, sporting a T-shirt that read *Beam Me Up Scotty, There's No Intelligent Life Down Here,* was keeping Bea and Yappy company. Newlin's beat-up pickup was parked on the outskirts of the gathering. He had apparently elected to stay inside the truck until midnight arrived.

"Are you sure you know what you're doing?" Charity asked for the fiftieth time.

"How hard can it be?" Elias led the way between two rows of RVs. "Breaking and entering is not what you'd call a high-tech profession. At least, not the way I plan to do it."

"What if you get caught?"

"I'll think of something."

"I don't like it."

"I told you to wait in the car."

She scowled at his sleek back. "I'm not going to let you handle this alone."

"Then stop whining."

"I'm not whining." She pulled the collar of her jacket higher around her neck and peered anxiously into the foggy darkness between two trailers. "I'm merely attempting to bring an element of common sense to this situation."

"It sure sounds like whining."

That did it. Charity set her teeth. She had used every reasonable argument she could think of to dissuade him from this reckless project. And he had the nerve to accuse her of being a whiner. She vowed she would not say another word on the subject, not even if he got himself arrested and called her to bail him out of jail.

Elias turned down a narrow, grassy aisle between two rows of campers and came to a halt with no warning. Charity stumbled against him with a muffled gasp. He reached out to steady her.

"Quiet," he whispered into her ear.

Charity shoved hair out of her eyes and leaned around him to see what had brought him to a sudden stop. She recognized Rick Swinton's maroon and white motor home parked in the last line of RVs.

"Change your mind?" she asked hopefully.

"No. Someone else got there first."

Charity stared at the darkened windows. "Are you sure?"

"Watch that rear window."

She studied the dark glass. A dim light shone briefly against the drawn curtains and then vanished. A moment later it reappeared for a few seconds. Charity swallowed.

"Flashlight?" she whispered.

"Yes."

"But it can't be Swinton. He's down on the beach with the others. We saw him join the crowd a few minutes ago."

"Right. Besides, Swinton wouldn't be using a flashlight in his own motor home."

Charity felt her mouth drop open. She closed it hurriedly. "My God. Someone else is in there doing just what you planned to do."

"It'll be interesting to see who comes out of there." Elias shifted position and pulled Charity into the small space between a trailer and a large camper.

She winced when her knee struck the trailer hitch. "Damn."

"Quiet. Whoever is in there is leaving." He eased her deeper into the shadows.

The door of the motor home squeaked as it opened. A figure in a hooded coat appeared and quickly went down the two steps to the ground. Charity tried to make out the face of the intruder, but the hood and the foggy darkness combined to make identification impossible.

The figure turned and hurried down the lane between two rows of RVs. The route would take the intruder straight past the spot where Charity and Elias stood.

Elias pressed Charity against the side of the trailer. She realized that he was using his body to shield her in case the fleeing figure glanced back into the shadows.

She stood on tiptoe to see over the barrier of Elias's arm and managed to catch another glimpse of the cloaked figure. There was something in the way the intruder moved that told her she was watching a woman flee the scene.

Elias waited a long moment before he shifted to release Charity. "Curiouser and curiouser."

"You can say that again." Charity was violently aware of her own pulse. "I wonder who she was."

"I have a feeling that Swinton has all kinds of enemies. I'd better get in and out before someone else shows up to take a look around." Elias stepped away. "Wait here."

"You're not going in there alone."

"I need you outside to keep watch."

That sounded reasonable. Charity couldn't think of a good counterargument. "Well, what should I do if I see someone?"

"Knock once on the outside wall of the motor home." Elias took one last look around the fog-shrouded scene as he removed a pencil-slim flashlight from the pocket of his jacket. "I'll be right back."

"If you don't come out of there in five minutes, I'll come in and drag you out."

Elias's teeth flashed briefly in the darkness. "Okay." He moved toward the door of the motor home.

Charity leaned around the corner to watch as he went up the steps and let himself inside.

A chilling silence descended when Elias disappeared. It seemed to Charity that the fog grew heavier. She told herself that was a good thing because it helped conceal Elias's shockingly illegal activities.

The chants from the beach intensified. The drums and flute played louder. The shouts and laughter of the watching teenagers drifted across the campground.

There was no sound from inside Swinton's motor home. No light was visible at the windows. Whatever Elias was doing, he was doing with great discretion. Charity shivered, partly from the chill and partly from increasing anxiety. The oppressive sense of impending danger thickened together with the fog.

Down below on the beach, the drummer went into a lengthy riff that carried clearly up the side of the bluff. The throbbing, pulsating chants of the excited Voyagers echoed loudly. Someone honked a horn. The teenagers' raucous laughter grew more strident. Charity heard the snap and pop of firecrackers.

After what seemed hours, the motor home door cracked open. Relief washed through Charity when she saw Elias jump lightly to the ground. He came toward her, moving with swift, silent grace.

"Come on, let's get out of here." He took her arm.

She didn't argue. "You were in there forever. Did you find anything?"

"Maybe."

She glanced at him as he hurried her through the maze of silent recreational vehicles. "What's that supposed to mean?"

"I got some bank account numbers. Ever notice how people tend to let their bank statements pile up in a desk drawer?"

"No." Charity hesitated, recalling the stack of statements she had filed in a desk drawer at home. "On second thought, maybe I have noticed. What of it? What good are the account numbers?"

"I don't know yet." Elias paused at the intersection of two lanes of campers. "But with an operation this big, you know everything is going through a bank."

"Hmm. You're right."

More firecrackers popped in the darkness. The Voyagers' chants reached a feverish pitch. The rowdy males who had gathered to drink beer near the bluff path began calling loudly down to the people on the beach. The younger set jeered and shouted.

"Things are getting exciting," Elias remarked as they moved out from behind the last row of vehicles.

"It's almost midnight." Charity glanced around. "And surprise, surprise, not a spaceship in sight. Let's go find Newlin. I want to be with him when the time comes, just in case Arlene doesn't rush into his arms."

"Right."

They made their way along the bluff to where Newlin had parked his pick-up. The battered truck was located in the outermost section of the makeshift parking lot. Nearly everyone else who had driven out to watch the spectacle had parked much closer to the campground.

The pickup was almost invisible in the fog. Charity went to the window on the driver's side and frowned when she saw that Newlin was not inside.

"He must have gone to the fence to wait for Arlene to come back from the beach," Elias said.

"Yes." The brief, sharp blast of an automobile horn made Charity jump. Someone cursed.

She turned and saw that there was one other vehicle parked a short distance away. Another truck. The passenger door was open, but there was no light inside the cab. The sound of the town's one and only rock station spilled forth into the night.

"Damn it," someone muttered from inside the truck. "I told you to be careful. You want someone to hear us?"

"The guy in the pick-up just left." There was a muffled giggle from the interior of the vehicle. "Speaking of careful, I hope you remembered the rubber. Because if you didn't, I swear to God, Kevin, you can go fly a kite tonight."

"Yeah, yeah. I've got it here, somewhere. Hang on."

Charity turned quickly back to Elias and cleared her throat. "Let's see if we can find Newlin." She grabbed his arm and started to lead him back the way they had come.

There was enough light reflecting off the fog to see Elias's amused expression, but he did not resist the forceful tug on his arm.

Charity pulled him toward the group that had gathered at the rail.

An eerie, startling hush descended on the group down on the beach. The flute and drum fell silent. The chants of the Voyagers ceased.

"Midnight," Elias said softly.

"Hey there, Charity. Winters." Yappy hailed them as they went past the tailgate refreshment stand. "We're gettin' ready to close up here. Want some hot coffee?"

"No, thanks," Elias called. "We're looking for Newlin."

"Saw him about an hour ago. Took some coffee over to his truck. Haven't seen him since."

"Everyone's gone to the fence to see the grand finale," Bea said as she packed a stack of unused paper cups back into a box. "Check over there. Sure hope Arlene comes to her senses tonight. If she doesn't, I don't know what poor Newlin's going to do with himself."

Charity turned toward the large crowd that was hovering over the fence, watching the scene on the beach. "Elias, I'm worried. I don't see Newlin anywhere."

He wrapped his hand around hers. "We'll find him."

That was going to be easier said than done, Charity thought. An air of confusion was building swiftly. Between the fog and the throng of excited, curious onlookers, things were becoming chaotic. Derisive shouts went up from the beer drinkers. The teenagers hooted as some of the Voyagers began to climb back up the beach path.

Charity and Elias moved through the clustered townsfolk, searching for Newlin. There was no sign of him anywhere.

"Hey," one of the beer drinkers yelled to the returning Voyagers, "Maybe the aliens meant Eastern Daylight Savings Time, not Pacific Daylight Savings Time."

The dispirited cult members filed past without acknowledging the taunts.

A high, shrill scream ripped through the darkness

just as Charity was about to suggest that they start looking for Arlene among the returning Voyagers.

The piercing shriek had the same impact on the crowd as a sky full of alien spaceships. Everyone, Voyagers and onlookers alike, froze.

Charity glanced around wildly, searching for the screamer. "One of the disappointed Voyagers, do you think?"

"I don't know. But it didn't come from the beach." Elias's hand tightened on hers. "It came from over there near the far end of the campground." He started forward.

A second cry reverberated through the night.

"What's going on?" Someone yelled. "Who's screaming?"

For the second time that night Charity allowed Elias to draw her into the maze of campers, motor homes, and trailers that littered the old campground. The screams were replaced by shouts for help.

"Someone call an ambulance," a man yelled. "For God's sake, hurry."

Charity and Elias emerged from between a row of camper trucks and saw that a handful of Voyagers who must have been among the first to return from the beach had gathered at the entrance to a large blue and white RV.

"That's Gwendolyn Pitt's motor home," someone said.

As she and Elias drew closer, Charity saw that light blazed from the open door of the vehicle.

Elias forged a path through the small crowd.

"It was because the ships didn't come," a woman dressed in Voyager's garb moaned. "She did it because the ships didn't come."

Charity saw Newlin and Arlene standing arm-in-arm

at the edge of the small cluster of people gathered outside the motor home. "Newlin."

He glanced at her. There was a peculiar expression of stunned shock on his face. "Charity. Mr. Winters. You aren't gonna believe what's happened."

Arlene buried her face against Newlin's shoulder. "It wasn't her fault the ships didn't come."

Elias released Charity's hand. "Wait here." He went up the steps to look inside the motor home. He came to a halt in the doorway, gazing intently at something inside.

Charity followed him up the steps and glanced past him into the interior of the motor home.

She took one look and immediately wished that she had followed Elias's orders to wait outside.

Gwendolyn Pitt was sprawled on the blue carpet. Her blue and white robes were drenched in blood. Rick Swinton was pressed back against the built-in desk, staring down at the body. He looked up and saw Elias and Charity.

"We just found her like this," he said in a shaken voice. "A few of us came back here to see why she hadn't joined us down on the beach. And we found her like this. I sent someone to call an ambulance. Not that it will do any good."

Without a word, Elias crossed the short distance and crouched beside the body. He pressed his fingers against the side of Gwendolyn's throat and shook his head.

"You're right," Elias said quietly. "It's too late."

"She must have killed herself because the space-ships didn't come," someone whispered.

Elias met Charity's eyes. "This wasn't suicide."

9

※

Blood in the water clouds the reflections on the surface, making it difficult to see the truth.

—"On the Way of Water," from the journal of Hayden Stone

"Murdered." Radiance leaned over Yappy's shoulder to read the article on the front page of the *Cove Herald*. "But last night everyone was saying that it was suicide."

Bea gave Charity a meaningful look as she handed her a latte. "Not everyone."

Yappy frowned as he scanned the article. "It says those who reached the scene first assumed Gwendolyn Pitt took her own life because she was despondent over the failure of the ships to arrive at midnight. But Hank Tybern states that it was obvious to him from the start that it was murder."

"It was obvious to Elias, too." Charity sipped her tea and glanced at the faces of the others who were

175

gathered around the small table inside the Whispering Waters Café. "Besides, none of us really believed that Gwendolyn Pitt actually expected the ships to arrive. We all suspected the whole operation was a scam. So why would she kill herself because of despair and disappointment?"

"Good point. Things went just the way she had planned." Ted scratched his broad belly, which today was partially concealed behind a gray T-shirt decorated with the words *What Goes Around, Comes Around*. "She was into that cult thing for something besides a tour of the galaxy. Pretty clear she was murdered. But who would have killed her?"

"Seems to me Chief Tybern has himself a whole slew of suspects," Yappy said. "Starting with all those disappointed Voyagers who must have realized at about one minute after midnight last night that they'd been conned."

Charity and the others nodded solemnly in agreement and sipped their morning lattes.

They had congregated inside Bea's café because it was too chilly to be outdoors. The fog that had descended on the cove showed no signs of lifting. It cloaked the entire town and the shoreline for several miles.

It was nine-thirty. The pier shops wouldn't open until ten, but all of the shopkeepers had arrived early by unspoken consensus to rehash the previous night's events.

All but one, Charity thought. She glanced out the window. There was still no sign of Elias. She hadn't seen him since he had left her at her door at two o'clock that morning. He hadn't even kissed her good night. He had been back in his cryptic mode, distant, remote, self-contained.

Of course, she hadn't been in what anyone could

call a cheerful mood herself last night. Her short stretches of restless sleep had been poisoned with instant replays of the horrifying scene inside Gwendolyn's motor home. Every time she closed her eyes, she was forced to endure the image of Elias crouched beside the blood-soaked body.

She was becoming increasingly uneasy by his failure to show up early at the pier. She wished she had followed her first impulse and stopped by his cottage on her way to work. The two of them needed to talk. They had to get their stories straight.

They had both spoken to Hank Tybern, the town's chief of police, last night, but the conversation had been necessarily brief. Hank had had his hands full securing the crime scene and warning the confused, anxious Voyagers not to leave town. There hadn't been time to take complete statements. He had instructed Charity and Elias to come by the station later today so that they could give him the details of what they had seen.

When she hadn't been dreaming about blood during the night, Charity had lain awake fretting over what to tell Hank this afternoon. She had never been involved in a police investigation. She had no idea how much information she and Elias would be expected to provide concerning their activities before the murder. With luck, not much. After all, they hadn't even been the ones to discover the body. Rick Swinton and a small group of Voyagers had done that.

Nevertheless, she had seen enough crime shows on television to guess that Tybern would want to know something about what had been happening in and around the campground prior to Gwendolyn's death. And there was no getting around the fact that she and Elias had been engaged in a highly questionable activity shortly before the murder. Namely, a spot of B and E. How did one put a respectable gloss on that kind of thing, she wondered.

"Does the article say when Gwendolyn was killed?" Ted asked.

Yappy read through the remainder of the lengthy piece. "The chief is waiting for the official results of the autopsy, but the reporter says that it appears she was shot between eleven-thirty, which is when she was last seen alive, and midnight. Swinton and a few of the Voyagers found her body a few minutes after twelve."

"That's when the screaming started," Bea said.

"I'll bet the county medical examiner won't be able to nail down the time of death any closer than that," Ted said, with the ghoulish authority of a devoted aficionado of the mystery genre. "Who was the last one to see her alive?"

"I think it was that Rick Swinton character." Yappy ran his forefinger along the column and paused midway. "Yeah. Rick Swinton and a couple of Voyagers. They all saw Gwendolyn go into her motor home at eleven-thirty. She told them she needed privacy in order to focus her mind channel for the aliens. Apparently she was supposed to act as their radar control for the landing."

"Well, if you ask me," Bea said, "I'll put my money on one of those Voyagers as the murderer. A lot of those poor, misguided souls lost their entire life savings to Gwendolyn Pitt."

"At least a few of them must have been furious last night when the ships didn't show," Radiance said.

"Yeah." Yappy put down the paper and picked up his latte cup. "And just about any one of 'em could have killed her."

Ted scowled. "If it was a Voyager, he or she would have had to work fast. They were all down there on the beach until the stroke of midnight. The kids hanging around the fence saw the first ones return."

"Don't forget, there are two beach access paths," Yappy reminded him. "The old one's been blocked off for years because it's unsafe, but it's still there."

"That's right." Ted brightened. "And there was a lot of fog last night. One of those Voyagers could have climbed up the old beach path, gone straight to Gwendolyn's motor home, shot her, and then rejoined the crowd on the beach. No one would have noticed because of the fog. The killer could have returned to the campground with the main group shortly after midnight."

"This is beginning to sound complicated," Bea muttered. "When you think about it, any one of those Voyagers could have done it that way. Couldn't tell them apart in the fog what with those blue and white hooded robes they all wear."

"I sure don't envy Chief Tybern," Ted said sagely. "Hell of a job sorting out this mess."

"Especially given his lack of experience," Radiance murmured dryly. "We haven't had a murder in Whispering Waters Cove in over ten years. And the last one was easy to solve, remember?"

Ted nodded. "Right. That was the time Tom Frazier's wife finally got fed up with old Tom beatin' up on her. She conked him on the head with a tire iron. Jury called it self-defense."

"Which it most certainly was," Bea added. "That Tom was a real sonofabitch."

The door of the café slammed open. The crash riveted everyone's attention. Charity and the others turned to see Arlene Fenton, breathless, disheveled, and obviously on the thin edge of rising panic. She flew into the café and then came to a quivering halt. Her wide-eyed gaze went straight to Charity.

"Ms. Truitt, thank God," she breathed in a shaky voice. "I went to your house, but you weren't there. And you weren't at your shop. I finally realized you must be in here."

"Arlene." Charity put down her latte and got to her feet. "What is it? What's wrong?"

"You have to save him. You have to save Newlin."

"Newlin? Calm down, Arlene." Charity started toward her. "Tell me what happened."

"Chief Tybern arrested Newlin a few minutes ago."

There was a collective gasp of shock from the small group gathered in the café.

"Oh, my God," Charity whispered. "Not Newlin."

Arlene rushed toward Charity with a stricken expression. "Ms. Truitt, what are we going to do? Everyone in town knows how much Newlin hated Gwendolyn Pitt. He was always saying that someone should do something about her."

Charity put her arms around her and looked at the other shopkeepers.

No one said a word. Arlene was right. Everyone in town knew that Newlin had been enraged by Gwendolyn Pitt's scam.

"He didn't do it," Arlene wailed. "I know he didn't. Newlin's no murderer. But he's got no one to help him."

"I'll go down to the station and talk to Chief Tybern," Charity said quietly.

Not that she had any notion of what to say to the chief, Charity thought, as she walked up the steps of the small Whispering Waters Cove Police Station twenty minutes later. Newlin was her employee and her friend. She felt she had to help.

Mentally, she started to tick off an action item list. The first thing to do, obviously, was see about getting